THE BUTTERCUP
FIELD

THE BUTTERCUP FIELD

D J O'Leary

Matador
9 Priory Business Park,
Wistow Road, Kibworth Beauchamp,
Leicestershire, LE8 0RX
Tel: 0116 279 2299
Email: books@troubador.co.uk
Web: www.troubador.co.uk/matador
Twitter: @matadorbooks

ISBN 978 1789018 424

British Library Cataloguing in Publication Data.
A catalogue record for this book is available from the British Library.

Printed and bound in Great Britain by 4edge Limited
Typeset in 11pt Filosofia by Troubador Publishing Ltd, Leicester, UK

Matador is an imprint of Troubador Publishing Ltd

Dedicated to the memory of the late Eric Hill,
the Somerset stalwart, who sowed the seed.

PROLOGUE

It was an unseasonably warm night in late February. There was no frost, and, crucially, no moon. The church clock had just struck for the twelfth time, and before the echoes of that final chime had faded, and almost as if it had been a cue, a shadow detached itself from the dark edges of the field and began to move furtively towards the far corner, the whole time hugging the hedge that ran along the roadside. This intrigued Ned Kincaid, who was sitting on the ground at the other end of the Buttercup Field, his back against a large and ancient oak tree.

After perhaps a minute and a half, during which time whoever it was moved stealthily into and out of the deeper darkness along the margins, it finally came to a halt at the top of the field. There was definitely something shifty about it, thought Ned. Whoever it was clearly did not want to take any chances and run the risk of being discovered, to judge by the clandestine approach. Yet, despite the paucity of light, the person appeared to move with confidence, as if he or she was wearing night vision goggles, or, far more likely, was very familiar with the terrain.

Ned shifted his backside as the cold damp in the ground began to penetrate his thick corduroy trousers. He knew he should make his way home, but ever since his wife Gladys had died he had felt less and less like spending time in the modest tied cottage that he had called home for the best part of three quarters of a century. Instead he had found himself more inclined to while away the evenings in his favourite corner of the public bar, sipping glass after glass of local cider, as he had done for as far back as he could remember, and certainly since he had first started work as a farm labourer, aged fourteen. As old as he was, and these days not even Ned was quite sure how old that was, there was little wrong with his vision; he was a countryman after all, and he had spent many nights out in the fields and the woods doing this or that. So he did not miss the secretive movement. He followed its progress, his curiosity piqued, although not unduly so; folks did do strange things, especially in these modern times, and it was probably none of his business.

He could not help but wonder just what might be going on at midnight, in the middle of what was supposed to be winter. For its part the figure might have wondered just what Ned was doing out in the field at this time of night. In fact, he invariably paused here on his way home, had done so for many years. It was his way of clearing his head after an evening in the pub. He would sit for anything up to an hour, absorbing the nocturnal sounds around him.

By now he could only just make out the figure. It seemed to be crouching in the far corner, the one nearest the road, where the shadows were at their deepest. Old Ned adjusted his position once more, easing himself higher by using the trunk of the oak tree. He considered making a discreet exit from the field while the person was engrossed in whatever it was doing, but he decided that his movement might be spotted, and if the person were someone prone to violence, they might think nothing of clobbering an old man such as Ned. He decided to sit it out.

As things turned out he did not have to wait all that long. Whatever it was that the person had been doing had occupied them for only a couple of minutes. Ned realised that he could now see the figure beginning the return journey to the spot where it had originally entered the field. Ned gave the person a further five minutes to get clear before he got to his feet. There had been no sound of a car engine starting up, so Ned concluded that the person had to have been a local. He further reasoned that if the person were on foot then he or she had to be given plenty of time to get clear of the field. Finally, quietly and carefully, he worked his way around to his right, keeping tight to the hedge line, just as the mysterious figure had done. Ned was cautious in his movements, worried that if he stepped on a twig and it snapped, that if the person were still nearby, they would hear it.

His caution meant that in all it took Ned almost five minutes to reach the spot where he judged the person to have been; he was not too sure of the place, but was certain that he was close. The trouble was that, despite his countryman's eyesight, it was so dark in the overhang of the trees and the hedges at this end of the field that an owl would have struggled to see anything. The spot had been well chosen, and again it occurred to Ned that this clandestine operation must have been well planned and possibly rehearsed. Ned squatted slowly, his knees creaking and cracking. Once down he thrust out a hand and began to pass it lightly over the surface of the ground, not sure what he was searching for, but convinced that if there was anything to be found it would become evident to him. The surface seemed to be devoid of dead leaves and twigs and grass. Instead what he could feel was earth. Fresh earth, smoothed down. Something had been buried here. But it had to be something small, because the area of newly-raked and tamped-down earth was perhaps two hands' breadths, no more. Without a torch and some sort of implement Ned did not want to disturb the site any further, but he decided it might be worth returning during daylight to conduct a more thorough search. Except, he mused, how could he do that without being seen? He pondered it for a second or two, then decided that it probably was not worth the effort. Whatever had been buried there was none of his business. And like as not, the mystery would eventually be solved anyway, as these things invariably were. It was practically impossible to keep a secret in small communities such as this.

He eased himself painfully back to his feet, his knees popping and protesting again as he did so. He might consider himself a countryman, thought Ned wryly, but he had to remind himself that he was an old countryman. At last, just as cautiously as he had arrived, he left the spot, carefully retracing his steps. He had drawn almost level with the gateway that opened onto the road when he heard a scuffling noise and a whispered curse, accompanied by some wheezy breathing. His initial thought was that the mystery person had returned. Ned froze. He was a few yards from the hedge and the only real cover he had was the darkness. He waited.

Clearly no one had spotted him, and he could not see anyone either. He remained as still as stone. After perhaps half a minute he heard the distinct sound of a spade being driven into earth. A pause, a wheezy breath, then another sound of the spade. It sounded as if they were right by the gate. This went on for a further minute, with whoever was wielding the spade wheezing repeatedly. *If I'm not mistaken there's only one man who wheezes like that in the village, and that's Clem Pewsey*, Ned thought to himself.

The sound of the spade stopped and Ned heard someone whisper, 'That'll do.' Then, half a minute after that, 'Put it back carefully.' Another pause, then the sound of earth being pounded, and finally, 'Right, let's go.'

Ned decided that this could not be the original person. In fact, he felt sure that he had seen two shadows crossing the gate entrance when the digging was done. And furthermore, there appeared to be a conversation going on, albeit one-sided. And if there were two of them and if one of them was Clem Pewsey, then it was a dead cert that the other one was Scott Ritching. They worked for a wealthy local farmer and were practically inseparable. Ned certainly did not want to reveal his presence to them, or indeed to anyone, although he was curious as to what had gone on in the second incident. But that would have to wait. He felt sure that the second incident was something to do with the gate, and he was equally certain that he would be able to spot anything unnatural in its look in daylight. Quietly he went all the way up to the oak tree, then past it, before slipping through the gap in the hedge which brought him back out opposite the pub. Lights were still on inside, but Ned would not get a drink now, and anyway he had had enough cider for one night. He had also had enough of shadowy figures. It seemed the world had gone mad. It was bad enough having one person acting secretively, but for there to have been two more was almost too much for Ned. It was definitely time for him to head home to his empty cottage.

ONE

It was threatening to turn into a summer of record high temperatures and hosepipe bans, when England would almost certainly be transformed from a green and pleasant land to parched yellow or scorched brown earth, courtesy of the unremitting sunshine and drastically reduced ozone layer. It had not rained for nine weeks, and now, in mid-July, farmers and gardeners, nurserymen and landscape designers were at their collective wits' end as they tried to protect stock, crops and herbaceous borders from the predatory drought.

Out of the shimmering heat, in the early afternoon of this sweltering Saturday high in the Weald of Kent, there emerged the figure of a young man, toting a leather holdall in his left hand and dragging his feet in their dust-covered shoes uphill away from the railway station. At the summit of the hill the sweaty figure, who went by the name of Warren Pearce, although he was known almost universally as "Tolstoy", came to a halt on his hike and leaned exhaustedly and momentarily on a five-barred gate, to mop his brow and take a breather, before continuing the trek. He was faced with a choice at this juncture in his journey. Just ahead of him, about fifty yards further on, and on the opposite side of the road, was a pub, the Snitcher's Head, a venue with which he was acquainted. He thought longingly of its cool dark interior and the soothing pint of beer he could savour and swallow were he to go there now. To his right, through the gate on which he had just propped his weary frame, and beyond a further gate some one hundred yards distant, lay his destination, the Stottenden village cricket ground. He could, of course, have headed straight for the cricket field, but thirst and a pressing desire for somewhere to cool off, albeit momentarily, won him over. So, after glancing back at the way he had come, up a narrow country lane, which fed into one only slightly larger, before veering downhill to the railway station, and finally ending at the junction with the major road that led to the South Coast, he made his move. Eventually, opening the heavy old oak door of the hostelry he stepped inside and crossed to the bar.

There was a youngish woman serving, although there was only one other customer at that time of day, unsurprising since there was a cricket match involving pretty well all able and less able-bodied adults in the village. The solitary customer was an old boy, nursing a pint of local cider, and he was one of the oldest inhabitants of Stottenden, Ned Kincaid. Tolstoy recognised the barmaid, a woman around his own age, perhaps late twenties, maybe even thirty. She was called Joanna Fordham, a pretty, dark-haired woman of average height. She was a local and seemed to pop up everywhere. On his last visit he had encountered her delivering newspapers early in the morning, and later on that same day she had served him in the village shop, before drawing him a pint of his favourite Fuggles bitter in the evening. When he had asked her if she was a workaholic she had replied that she was saving up to leave the village and start a new, more exciting, life up in London, so she needed to take on as many jobs as she could physically manage. Other locals had told him that Jo, as she was known, had been saving up for her "getaway" for as long as anyone could remember.

'Hello Mr Pearce, what'll it be?'

'Hello Jo – and it's Warren, or Tolstoy – could I have a pint of Fuggles, please?'

'Coming right up. It should be nice and cool, welcome on a hot day like this.' She took a pint mug from an overhead hook just above the bar and set it beneath the pump and began to draw the beer from the barrel.

Feeling a responsibility to sustain the conversation, Tolstoy ventured to sustain the dialogue. 'Yes, it's really hot out there, but this should slake my thirst.'

'What was that word? Slake?'

'Yes.'

'Is it the same as quench?'

'Yes.'

'Why not say quench then?'

'Because,' he felt slightly affronted, 'I prefer slake.'

'Oh well. You do tend to use posh words. But that's you, isn't it? At least that's what everyone who knows you says.'

She glanced up at him before wiping some stray drops of beer from his glass and placing it on the bar in front of him, then ventured, 'Stop me if I'm being too nosey, but I've always wondered, why are you known as Tolstoy?'

'Well, my name Warren Pearce sounds a little like *War and Peace*, the very long novel by the Russian author Leo Tolstoy. It was actually my father's little joke to call me Warren, then he knew he could have fun with my nickname, and family and friends have called me Tolstoy ever since.'

'Thanks for that. Do you mind being called Tolstoy?'

'No, at least, I'm so used to it now it is almost as if it were my given name.' He paused for a moment, then, following the tradition of all locals of the Snitcher's Head, Tolstoy added, 'Could you refill Ned's glass, please?' And he nodded in the direction of the other customer at the bar.

'Yes, of course,' said Jo and moved down the bar to where Ned was sitting, said a few words to him in an undertone, turned and pointed out Tolstoy, before picking up his by now empty glass and heading for the cider pump. She took the full glass back to the old man, who turned towards Tolstoy, nodded his head in appreciation before raising the glass to his lips and drinking a surprising amount in one go.

Tolstoy paid for the drinks, moved across to a table and sat down, and reflected on his journey, not least what had greeted him at the start of his walk to the centre of Stottenden village. On leaving the station, which was more a halt-whistle than a travel hub, he had faced a slog on foot of a country half-mile — all of it uphill — and for someone not used to walking, such as he, it had been a fair old hike in this heat. His route to his destination had been lined with placards on each side of the road, stating "Save Our Buttercup Field" in black letters on a yellow background. The placards were the symbol of a protest that had consumed the village since Jack Bentley, a local "gentleman" farmer, who also just happened to be the chairman of the parish

4

council, and was a man renowned for his overbearing and bullying manner, had decided to lay claim, on behalf of the council, to the Buttercup Field, which had immediately been earmarked for residential development. It had been the previous November that this shattering news had been made public, and rather puzzlingly for Tolstoy, at the time, his godfather Hubert de Groot had invited, nay insisted, that he come down from London for a chat about the Buttercup Field crisis – including attending a meeting of concerned villagers – and one or two other matters, which would all be explained on his arrival. On that occasion Tolstoy had also taken the train, but had been spared the long uphill hike in the November "mizzle" – that miserable drizzle which seemed able to penetrate even the most waterproof and snug of coats – that cloaked Kent late on that particular afternoon, by the appearance of his godfather's wife Elspeth, who had been there to meet him in her car, Stottenden not having a regular bus or taxi service from the station to the centre of the village.

On reaching Stottenden Manor Tolstoy had picked up his overnight bag from the back of the car and joined Elspeth as she opened the front door. It was an imposing, yet welcoming, house. The hall would have been gloomy had it not been for the thoughtful lighting of the vast area, whose focal point was the grand staircase that split left and right at the first landing, taking guests into one of the eight bedrooms that lay on the first floor. There was a second floor that had, in its day, housed servants, but for the most part now those modest rooms remained unused.

His godfather had been in the library, which lay to the left of the front door, and Elspeth led him to it. Hubert de Groot was sitting in a leather wingback chair, one that creaked with every movement, as Tolstoy knew, and over to his left a large log fire burned brightly.

De Groot looked up from the book he was reading. 'My dear Tolstoy, welcome.' He then hauled himself slowly and, to Tolstoy's eye, painfully out of his chair and held open his arms to greet his godson. Although appearing rather thin, pale and drawn, de Groot nevertheless still cut an imposing figure, topping six feet, and blessed with an abundance of white hair that crowned a lean, tanned face in which were set a pair of sharp grey eyes that had seen much in life and missed very little. He was, as usual, immaculately turned out, in a check shirt, sharply-creased slacks and highly-polished shoes.

His wife was also a picture of elegance. In her youth a beauty, now possibly even more alluring, life's experiences having left sympathetic tracks of the passage of time, rather than ravages. Elspeth was of aristocratic bearing, an aquiline nose set perfectly between deep blue eyes above and full lips below. Her figure was as good now as it had been when she and de Groot had first met, when she was in her late twenties and he in his late forties. 'A good journey down?'

'Excellent, Hubert. I love this last bit on the steam train.'

'Yes everyone loves it. It runs through some picturesque countryside and also through some varied farmland.'

'Yes, and it's lovely to see that hops have made a comeback after what happened at the end of the last century.'

Elspeth cut in, 'Tea?'

'Yes, please,' the men replied in unison, and de Groot, indicating the other wingback chair opposite his, said, 'Take a seat. There's a lot to discuss and the meeting I'd like you to attend as my representative starts at seven o'clock, so I think an explanation for my summoning you here is called for.'

Tolstoy sat, leaned back and focused on his godfather.

'I'd like to begin with a brief history of Stottenden Manor and village, so please bear with me,' he began. Tolstoy nodded.

De Groot began by explaining how Stottenden Manor House had come to be in the Dutch family's hands for close on half a millennium. Originally Flemish weavers, or, more accurately, clothiers, which was the wealthy end of the industry, the de Groots had settled in this part of Kent in the fourteenth century, as had so many of their fellow countrymen, thanks to an invitation by Edward III. The family had soon diversified and expanded their business. In addition to exporting Kentish cloth to the Continent, they began importing luxuries from overseas; initially their shipping business was based in Rye, where it boomed. As a result, over the next few centuries the de Groots became excessively wealthy, thanks to the burgeoning tea and spice trades, among other things. When sufficiently well-off they had had Stottenden Manor House constructed, having decided that they wanted to live somewhere that was a little removed geographically from their business activities, and the, then remote, clearing high in the Weald of Kent that was Stottenden seemed ideal. Work began on building Stottenden Manor House in the middle of the last decade of the late sixteenth century. The de Groots purchased a sizeable area of the woodland, siting their manor house on one edge, while creating a large garden and a field on the rest of the land. It was this field which eventually, some 150 years later, became the cricket field, a path leading directly onto it from the garden of the Manor House. At the time of the manor's construction Stottenden had been a hamlet, a clearing on a hill in the Weald of Kent, which served as grazing ground for cattle and pigs belonging to a handful of locals. But the de Groots decided that they wanted to ensure that Stottenden would grow into something grander, and in order to get that particular ball rolling, they had donated a breathtaking (for those times) sum of money to have a church, St Martin's, built in the village.

Not too long after that the odd cottage sprang up here and there, and eventually and inevitably the first alehouse appeared, after an enterprising, would-be publican saw the potential of the place. Sadly, within a few decades the alehouse had burned down, to be replaced, in the early eighteenth century, by the present building, which sported possibly the most macabre and grisly name for a hostelry in the whole of the county – the Snitcher's Head. Local legend had it that in those days, when smuggling was rife on the Kent and Sussex coast, that one righteous villager had tipped off the authorities about the suspicious activities and nocturnal comings and goings of a neighbour. A posse of revenue men had lain in wait and had caught the man, and a number of others, all of whom were members of a notorious gang of smugglers in that area, as they returned from the coast transporting a few cartloads of baccy, claret, lace, tea and other such luxuries. The episode did not end so well for the tipster, because, unfortunately for the "grass", one of the Customs and Excise men was in the pay of the gang of smugglers, and, on being informed of what had happened, a kangaroo court was held in the bar of the village inn; the man was found guilty by the gang members and he was sentenced to death by beheading. His head was duly separated from his body, then paraded around the area before being suspended from a tree that grew just outside the pub. Ever after the King's Arms, as it had once been called, came to be known as the Snitcher's Head.

The local history lesson over, Hubert got down to the business of the day. 'I asked you down here because there are a couple of things you need to know. Some good news and some not so good news. Firstly, after much thought and discussion with Elspeth and my solicitor, I have decided to leave you the house and grounds, including the cricket field, in my will.'

Tolstoy's jaw dropped and he stared at his godfather in shock. But before he could utter a sound Hubert continued, 'The reason is that Elspeth and I, having been unable to have a family of our own, have always regarded you as a surrogate son, even though we have not seen quite so much of you since you left university and began to pursue your career.

'Now if, as expected, Elspeth survives me, I should want you to let her carry on living here,' with a wave of his right arm he indicated his home, 'but I think you will need to pop down here a little more often over the next few months in order for me to show you the ropes, because you need to know how things are run around here.'

As his godfather paused for breath, Tolstoy leapt in. 'Hubert? Are you sure? I mean, it's... it's... it's too much. Surely you have someone else you can leave it to? Someone in the family? A niece? A nephew? A cousin?' His voice trailed off as he saw his godfather shake his head.

'Disappointingly, no. But, as I have said, as far as we are concerned, you're as good as family, and anyway, you're the only person to whom I could entrust all of this. For one thing, perhaps the most important thing, you love your cricket, in fact you are as passionate about it, especially at this level, as I am. Therefore I'm confident that you will safeguard its traditions and its very existence. I know you'll take good care of the house and its history. And Elspeth and I hope that, in time, you will meet someone and marry them and I hope you will be more fortunate than Elspeth and I have been, and that you will be blessed with children in whom you will be able to instil the sense of history and traditions of Stottenden, and to whom you can, in your turn, bequeath everything that I am leaving you.'

Tolstoy sat back, dazed at the news. Excited as well, yet profoundly saddened too. 'Why have you decided on this now, Hubert? And why tell me now?'

'Why now? Well, that's the not so good news that I mentioned. It would appear that I have inoperable cancer. I shan't go into details, but there is quite a poor prognosis, not helped by my age. That's why I'm absolutely certain that Elspeth will survive me, apart from the fact that she is my junior by quite a few years, and is therefore commensurately fitter than I am.'

'Hubert, I'm so sorry. Isn't there anything the doctors can do?'

'Not a thing, I'm afraid. Not to worry though, I've had a good innings, and there is still time to enjoy a few months more of life and all that it has to offer. Not least this impending battle over the Buttercup Field.' The old man's face lit up momentarily at the prospect of the forthcoming fight. 'Could you explain it all to me, please?' asked Tolstoy.

'Gladly,' said Hubert.

'The parish council, under what I might say is the heavy hand of Jack Bentley – despite the fact that he has, quite properly, declared an interest and has absented himself from the parish council debate each time the matter has been raised – has opposed the majority of the locals and has recommended that the application be approved by the borough council. Indeed, the borough council had decided that there was a certain merit to the plan, because housing is in short supply in the area. Now, the thing is, Bentley has a business partner, a local builder and property developer, and this partner has promised that one third of the houses would be affordable starter homes to allow young locals a chance to remain in the village, where they had jobs. The borough council is determined not to rush into a decision, but the "carrot" of the starter homes certainly holds great appeal. So, after weeks of protests, including a sit-in in the council chamber, a lengthy petition and eventually some legal threats, the councillors have debated the matter at great length, and the issue is now delicately poised. They are on the brink of a decision. Of course the pessimistic Stottenden villagers expect the plans to be passed. Even the local press has been speculating that the borough council would give the plans the thumbs-up. In that eventuality the villagers have a number of objections they intend introducing. One of these is to claim that the Buttercup Field is, to all intents and purposes, a village green. There is certainly no other grassy area in Stottenden that remotely resembles such a facility.

'Everyone knows that were they to fail in their attempts then the matter would almost certainly go to central government and an inevitable public inquiry; were that to be the case then there would be no guarantee that a Home Office planning inspector would find for them. Indeed, the villagers were determined to avoid that step if at all possible.

'So it is up to everyone to put forward a convincing enough case to demonstrate that the Buttercup Field has been used for more than twenty years, in fact a lot more than twenty years, as a village green.'

Tolstoy was familiar with the Buttercup Field and its recent history. While not a resident himself, he had been a regular enough visitor to the village over the years, indeed since childhood, to be well acquainted with the Buttercup Field and its history.

Its barely three skinny acres – he happened to know just how big it was – had long since been adopted by the whole community as a sort of village green, or common land. It had staged parties, barbecues, car boot sales, and had acted as an overflow car park for cricket matches. It was also the only direct access to the cricket field from the road, and countless thousands of feet over some two hundred plus years had worn a path across it; a footpath which had then been straddled by the tyre tracks of innumerable vehicles, as generations of the village's cricketers and their opponents had headed to the picturesque sporting arena on the other side of the far hedge. It was also somewhere that the locals traditionally liked to stroll of a summer's evening, to take in the air and perhaps sit for a while in the long grass of summer and admire the spectacular view across the Weald. Hubert had paused briefly, then, leaning forward with a deep frown on his forehead, he added, 'There is something that is a little bothersome, not to say disturbing. It would appear that no one knows who owns the Buttercup Field. There don't seem to be any title deeds anywhere, therefore no one could challenge anyone else's claim to ownership of it. Naturally, this whole thing has caused an uproar. The village, indeed the whole of the surrounding area, is outraged. The council claims that it has been responsible for the upkeep of the Buttercup Field, mowing the grass verge running along the roadside of it, and trimming the hedgerows on a regular basis, and therefore has something they termed loosely as "husbandry rights", which means after a certain amount of time they can stake a claim to ownership of it. This is arrant nonsense and patently untrue. It has always fallen to the lot of the locals, farmers in the main, to trim the hedges, clear the roadside ditch, and occasionally to mow the field itself.

'Furthermore this claim of ownership has been challenged by a couple of legal people who live locally. One of them is a barrister, Angela Smeaton, who actually lives in the village. She says that the PC can have no legal claim to it, and that furthermore, no court in the land would uphold the council's case, because of the Buttercup Field's role over the years to the community here.'

Tolstoy interrupted the flow. 'But hang on, Hubert, the Buttercup Field adjoins the cricket field, which belongs to Stottenden Manor, and therefore to you. Surely that means the Buttercup Field belongs to you.'

His godfather gave a resigned little shrug. 'Sadly, my dear chap, that's not the case. As I've said we, that's to say my solicitor and his team, have scoured every scrap of paper, every document that has anything to do with Stottenden Manor, in the hope that at some later date one of my ancestors purchased the land then gave it to the village, or even the church. It had always been the general belief throughout my childhood, that a great-great-great whatever grandfather, in gratitude for all that the villagers had done, had made a gift of the field to the village. But it seems no one else, neither the church, nor the council, no one, has any record of any such thing having taken place. Now, thanks to Jack Bentley, the council, wrongly in my view, is claiming ownership of the land, oh of course, "on behalf of" the villagers. This whole thing smells, of money. I am urging our legal chaps to look into the establishment of common land, or something similar, but so far, nothing.'

'Has the proposal gone through all the planning processes?' asked Tolstoy.

'Not quite. But rumours are rife that the borough council, while it will happily prevaricate for a while and go through the motions of examining the various claims and counter-claims, will ultimately almost certainly come down on the side of Jack Bentley and his parish council.'

Tolstoy cocked his head on one side. 'Seems to be a lot of waiting around. Are there any grounds for not developing the site?'

'Well, if it were declared a site of special scientific interest, if there were proof of rare, indigenous species, be they insects, birds, reptiles, mammals or plants. Or, of course, if it is deemed to be a village green.'

'Surely that is precisely what it is,' said Tolstoy. 'It has staged fetes, the cricket club frequently uses it as an overspill car park, plus it provides the only public access to the cricket ground. And doesn't the church "borrow" it as a car park for christenings, weddings, funerals and the like?'

'Yes, it does. But the thing is,' de Groot raised himself a little and leaned forward in his chair, 'the cricket ground, being privately owned, cannot be entered into the equation. The council would argue that if access is needed to it, then the public should use the one here, at the Manor, since the cricket field is within the curtilage of Stottenden Manor, except that not many people would be prepared to park along the road and then walk, possibly up to a quarter of a mile, in order to gain access to a field to watch a cricket match.

'Oh, and another thing the borough council is also trying to claim is that because the Buttercup Field is enclosed on all four sides, that as enclosed land it cannot be deemed to be a village green. It's a legal minefield, with claim, counter-claim and very little documented proof of anything. Thankfully the village now has an action committee, with a fair amount of professional expertise it can call on, including legal.'

He paused for a moment then added, 'So, because of your pending ownership of Stottenden, I felt it necessary for you at least to attend the meeting about the Buttercup Field. It does look desperate, but there is the odd glimmer of hope. I don't expect you to take an active part, simply because you live in London and you have your job, but I do think you need to be in at the start of things. As I say, all is not as bleak as it might appear.'

So Tolstoy had duly been co-opted onto the committee that had been set up to try to find ways of forestalling and eventually thwarting the proposed development, although Tolstoy made it very clear to everyone that he could offer very little in terms of practical help to the cause, given

15

that he lived in London and worked odd hours, including weekends. But, it was suggested, he might come up with ideas that could be adopted and adapted. He had felt heartened by this reaction, and more comfortable sitting around a table with them.

TWO

Now, three months later, in the cool of the bar in the Snitcher's Head, Tolstoy knew matters were coming to a head. He felt defeated. During his contemplation of the village's troubles, Tolstoy found that he had drained his pint of beer. He debated briefly buying another, but decided against it.

Right, time to go. He rose, picked up his holdall, grabbed the glass and set it on the bar on his way out, said a farewell to Jo, then to Ned, who appeared to be dozing on his bar stool, although the old man half turned, smiled and raised a hand before returning to his previous state and Tolstoy hauled open the heavy door to be hit by the wall of heat outside.

He looked at his watch and sighed. He had hoped to arrive much earlier than this, but train problems meant the cancellation of the one he had intended to catch, and as a consequence he had missed his connection at Paddock Wood, and by the time the next local train arrived he was more than two hours behind schedule. Any frustration that he had felt about the delays, however, had been swiftly dispelled by the train journey into deepest West Kent. The line had originally been one of those closed more than half a century earlier, and not so long ago there had been no railway line, or no station at Stottenden, at least, not a working one. The old building had been used as an outhouse and storage facility for the previous sixty-plus years after Dr Richard Beeching's axe had fallen on the "Hopping Line" as it had been known.

But ten years ago a government initiative, which had attracted private investment, had deemed that the "Hopping Line" should be restored in a move to help ease congestion on the roads and improve rural communities' links with towns in the area. It was a necessarily complex process, involving the re-purchase or re-leasing of land that had once belonged to British Rail or the former railway company. But local businesses had seen the sense in taking freight off the snarled-up roads and had chipped in generously; staggeringly, local law firms carried out the legal side of the transfer of title to the newly set-up Hopping Line Branch Railway Company in near record time, with unthinkably generous discounts to help expedite affairs; and an impressively large army of volunteers, as ever where such projects are concerned, ensured that nine years almost to the day that the restoration had commenced, it was duly completed. Now villagers along the route had ready access to Paddock Wood, Tonbridge and all stations north and south on the main line, as well as a host of old and new halt-whistles. (These were unscheduled stops, usually on branch lines, where the guard's whistle would let the engine driver know he had to stop at what was generally just a short platform with no buildings or railway staff.) The one at the bottom of the hill below Stottenden had proved to be a great community asset. It had been running now for several years, and Tolstoy had never tired of travelling down to Kent on it, which he did as frequently as his godfather invited him.

His destination lay beyond the five-barred gate, across the Buttercup Field, through another five-barred gate and into the cricket field. The match was well under way by now of course, and since it was one of the biggest fixtures of the season, it drew a large crowd numbering former players for the Guns, their families and friends and so on. The larger than usual number of spectators meant more cars, and so Tolstoy found himself negotiating a way through and among the vehicles parked in the Buttercup Field. Initially he could only hear the sounds of activity, but then, as Tolstoy reached the second gate, a timeless tableau unrolled before him.

He just had to pause again and reflect that sometime in the not too distant future all that lay before him was going to be his. It seemed like a dream for someone who had grown up with very little material wealth. Of course he had savings, but a disappointingly low salary demanded that he supplement it from time to time from his nest egg. He was an only child and was just four years old when his father, Bill Pearce, a bank manager, had died of a heart attack. It was Bill's idea to name him Warren, thus ensuring that his nickname would forever be Tolstoy. Bill had loved joking and was a fan of the Russian author. Warren's mother, Nora, had been at school with Elspeth and had kept in touch since then, attending Elspeth's wedding and popping down to Stottenden regularly, especially after Bill's death. Sadly, breast cancer had claimed Nora when Tolstoy was ten and a boarder at a prep school near Stottenden. Thankfully Nora had had the good sense, after being diagnosed, to make her sister Rosemary and her husband Philip the guardians of her son. Hubert de Groot insisted that he would underwrite his godson's education from prep school and on through university, although the proceeds of the sale of the Pearce family home were invested and provided, through a trust fund, finances for at least part of the school fees. Tolstoy came to love both his guardians and his godfather and Elspeth, who would have him to stay for parts of the school holidays. Throughout his schooldays he generally escaped bullying, despite his dyspraxia – a condition which affected his coordination and movement – which rendered him a figure of fun in sports. Thankfully he had been blessed with intelligence, academic discipline and a dry wit. If he could not help his peers with their prep, then he could at least get them laughing to take the sting out of any awkward situations and scrapes that he might get himself into from time to time. After prep school it was off to a minor public school in deepest Sussex, before going up to university to read maths. Finally, when he failed interview after interview for various jobs, he stumbled on an archive post, found the work straightforward, even if the hours were not, and that was where he was now. Right. Onward again, he thought.

Tolstoy leaned over the gate to release the stiffish latch; initially, though, the gate seemed reluctant to swing back and admit him. Indeed, it required a deal of exertion, which instantly had him dripping with sweat, to persuade it to yield. Finally the wooden structure creaked open under his persistent pressure and allowed him onto the outfield. He closed the gate behind him, sighed, then placed his bag at his feet to gaze at what for him was that old cliché, "a quintessentially English scene". Except for the fact that a very dry spring and now the mid-summer drought had taken their toll. From what he could discern of the cricket ground, the square looked to be on the point of being transformed into a network of cracked clay, having dried to a concrete-like hardness, while the outfield was bare in places and brown in many others. It was still recognisably a cricket ground. On the opposite side stood the pavilion, originally built early in the Victorian era, then subsequently adorned with successive additions to support it and improve its facilities, not just for the players, but for the spectators as well. It presented a charming if somewhat eccentric picture, not quite what one might have expected, but with the large gathering of spectators, the occasional ripple of applause, the thud of willow on leather, for Tolstoy it epitomised everything that an English summer in the countryside should be. He picked up his bag once more, steadfastly refusing to doff his Harris Tweed jacket, and began the tricky job of working his way around to where his godfather habitually positioned himself, just beyond the pavilion and protected by the overhanging branches of a horse chestnut tree. From the start of this, the final stage of his journey that day, he was struck by how crowded the ground was, then he recalled that this was the weekend of the traditional "Guns versus Beaters" match, which had its origins in the local shoot. It had developed into a rivalry that boasted a lengthy history, and attracted a remarkable cross section of society. He paused, removed an already damp handkerchief from his trouser pocket to mop his forehead and face, while contemplating the task that lay before him.

In order to reach the pavilion he would have to pick out a pathway through the dense sprawl of spectators. In front of him there lay a rich collection of the sleek and the chic, fast cars and pacy women littering the boundary's edge, the latter invariably and inevitably turning the fringes of the arena into centre stage with a gesture or a look; the gleaming elegance of the former attracting envious, but admiring, glances from those passing by. And draped carelessly among these models of perfection were knots of old school ties, young men, Tolstoy noted with mild disapproval, who invariably had a hand resting proprietorially on bonnet or buttock, or both when the opportunity presented itself.

They were lounging around in this part of the field, keeping themselves a little apart, while they alternately quaffed and quipped among themselves, quick to laugh, and loudly; they knew they were not there to look at anything, rather they were there to be looked at. They knew they were the beautiful people. Eternally youthful. Society's immortals, who would never know pain or penury, illness or infirmity.

The problem Tolstoy had was how to negotiate a way through these svelte women and athletic-looking young men, who in general were showing more interest in each other and their glasses of bubbly than in the cricket match unfolding at their backs. Tolstoy noted wryly that they had commandeered a section of the outfield that had a welcome area of shade, one that, because of the angle of the shaw, the narrow strip of woodland which ran along this edge of the cricket field, would remain in shadow for much of the afternoon. He knew none of them, and they, for their part, took little notice of him, an averagely built man of indeterminate age, maybe late twenties, perhaps a thirty-something. All they might have noted was that this appeared to be someone dressed beyond his years, also unfashionably, and, given the weather, most inappropriately.

In truth Tolstoy was beginning to regret the choice of the jacket, but his navy blazer was pure wool, and if anything, even hotter than the Harris Tweed. Thereafter he had little else to choose from in his simple wardrobe, neither of his suits being remotely right for a sporting occasion on a summer's afternoon. Even as he made his cautious way through the cool ranks before him, his fingers dithered and dallied around the buttons of his jacket, uncertain as to whether he should stop and peel it off, sling it over his shoulder and then resume his slow walk, or leave it on and suffer until he had arrived at his destination. He convinced himself that to stop and disrobe right then would probably end in embarrassment, because that was the way of things in his life. Something untoward was bound to happen, inevitably attracting unwanted attention, so he opted for the "do nothing approach". He had already concluded the same for his collar and tie. They were to remain tight to his throat, as ever. Rare was the day when he could be found in an open-neck shirt. Work expected a collar and tie, habit demanded them; even Saturdays and Sundays he would be found buttoned up and wound into a fat Windsor knot, his only concession at weekends being to sport something a little more colourful and less conservative, perhaps a polka dot pattern or a garishly striped one. Today's, for example, was a startling red and white stripe, one that, he noticed irritably, had contrived to allow itself to be flicked over his left shoulder at some point on his way to the ground. In a brief blaze of temper he tucked the loose tail of the tie into the waistband of his cavalry twill trousers, jabbed his now damp handkerchief deep into his left-hand pocket, then took a firmer grip on his holdall and began to pick a way as delicately as he could around and through all the bodies that sat and lay on the grass. A murmured 'Excuse me, please' or a muttered 'So sorry' worked, if not quite as efficiently as Aaron's rod when he parted the Red Sea, then at least well enough to produce, albeit reluctantly, a temporary path over legs, around hampers and between supine and prone bodies. Gratefully he eased through, uncomfortable under any brief scrutiny as he picked his way, clumsily and sweatily, through their chilled, perfumed ranks. He was ever mindful of his broad, brown and heavy shoes, which frequently had a way of turning his feet into uncontrollable, not to say lethal, weapons.

Tolstoy enjoyed cricket at all levels, but most especially village cricket, although he was by no means fanatical about it; he did not play the game, had not done so for many years, thanks to an inexplicable, although mild, form of dyspraxia, which had from very early on persuaded him to seek out other pursuits which could be better negotiated. So not since his second year at school had he made a complete idiot of himself with bat or ball. Summers therefore had been spent in the long jump pit, although the only jumping he did there was when he was startled awake from his afternoon nap by the games master on the prowl for slackers. Winters had seen him strolling around the cross country course, taking in nature, watching for fieldfares and redwings, and being rewarded for his alertness with the occasional glimpse of a sparrowhawk beating up along the hedgerows, zooming effortlessly up and over from either side of the hedge in a breathtaking aerobatic display calculated to flush finches from their hiding places and into the hawk's clutches. He was not, by any description, an ornithologist, and certainly not a twitcher, travelling at a moment's notice to farthest Cornwall or to the most remote point of the north in order to tick off an "accidental" or rarity, yet he was drawn to nature, and found himself more and more frequently using the miniature binoculars, purchased for cricket, when he was abroad in the countryside. This afternoon he would interrupt his erratic progress whenever he had the chance with a brief halt and a glance out to the middle to take in the action, where he noted, with a degree of pleasure, that every man involved in the match was in "whites" or creams. That, and the frequent muted applause reassured him that the traditions of the game and respect for it were still alive and thriving, at least in this part of rural England.

Whether consciously or not, Tolstoy had been working his way to the outside edge of the crowd, where the going was less complicated, but the nearer he drew to the pavilion the older the people were and the more deckchairs he encountered. Then threading his way through became much more of a lottery, because interspersed among the deckchairs were picnic parties whose members had eschewed formal seating and instead had set up on the grass, and Tolstoy gradually found himself becoming more and more hemmed in again, until he finally reached a dead end. There just seemed to be no way through. As he turned this way and that, looking for a gap, he found himself confronted by an ocean of red hair, a discovery which gave him something of a jolt, and a not unpleasant one at that. As he hovered over the hair he became aware of a delicious smell of perfume, an almost lemony, yet floral fragrance that was really rather heady. For a few moments he lingered there, partly because he was reluctant to disturb the owner of the hair and partly because he was enjoying the moment, half-closing his eyes and breathing it all in deeply. He need not have fretted about not disturbing the hair's owner though. That he had already managed. The feeling of foreboding he had harboured about his clumsy feet had become reality. His right foot had inadvertently settled heavily onto some of the lustrous locks, and when the owner sought to move her head, to try to discover what was going on, she found she could not, not without a deal of pain anyway, and upon experiencing the pain let out a shriek, half in agony, half in anger. Thus everyone in the vicinity turned to look first at the source of the noise, then at the cause. "The Cause" blushed a deep crimson and began sweating even more profusely. Worse, he found himself unable to utter a sound, so embarrassed was he. He was rendered mute for long, miserable seconds. All he could do was stare down at her vacuously, his foot unmoving, seemingly frozen to the spot. He was shocked to the core at what had happened, and was unable to think or speak, so the shoe remained in place and the mouth remained half-open, slack with sorrow, and disbelief, incapable of forming sounds or words.

The look with which she greeted him when he finally acted and lifted his foot, was withering, icy, even. His eventual, scratchily uttered, 'Terribly sorry,' did not seem to register with her. But her voice reached him and indeed carried further, to the appreciative audience that had gathered around. 'Why, thank you so much for freeing my hair. Perhaps you might watch where you place your feet in future. And it might be advisable to find a route with fewer obstructions to negotiate.' Although the phrasing seemed mild, the tone used would not have been out of place in the Arctic Circle. He cringed, shrivelling in mortification. He tried apologising again, but his muttered stutterings fell on vexed ears. The young woman simply gathered her hair and herself, got to her feet and turned disdainfully away from him. He, spotting the opening left by his victim's action, darted through it and away from the scene of his humiliation.

There were no more such incidents, mercifully, and, with a glance out to the middle where the cricketing action was taking place, in order to update himself on the state of play, he finally arrived at the pavilion, pausing before stepping onto its venerable verandah to turn once more and drink in the near timeless scene. All thoughts of his recent embarrassing encounter with the chestnut-haired woman fled, and he relaxed for the first time in a while.

Before he could enter the pavilion Tolstoy heard his name, his proper name, being called out. The source of the voice was on the far side of the pavilion. He scanned the sea of faces, the majority of which were deckchair-based, and at first recognised no one.

'Warren! Warren! Over here!'

It was Elspeth. She stood up to make it easier for him to spot where the two of them were.

Tolstoy stepped off the verandah, gratefully, and this time made a trouble-free, if tortuous, trip over to them, managing to avoid young children, bored with the match, chasing each other around and through the spectators.

It was Elspeth who greeted him first. 'Tolstoy, darling,' and she stepped forward to give him a hug. 'How are you?'

'Very well, if a little hot and dusty, perhaps. That's quite a walk from the station in this weather.'

'You should have let us know when you arrived, it would have been no trouble to get the car out and potter down to the station.'

'Oh, I had no idea what precise time I would be getting in, and as things turned out I managed to miss one train, the next was cancelled, so I'm at least a couple of hours behind schedule. I didn't want to bother you, drag you away from this. And that is just as well given the way things turned out. Anyway, the exercise may well have done me some good.'

'Well you're here now. When you've said your hellos to Hubert I shall take you over to the pavilion, Fiona Selby – do you remember Fiona? – anyway, she has made the most delicious lemonade. It's her grandmother's recipe and it is utterly refreshing.'

Tolstoy shook his godfather's hand, smiling. 'Hello Hubert. How are things?'

'So-so. The damned thing gets no better and it's bloody well spreading. But I'm still here. I wouldn't have missed this match for the world.'

And Tolstoy nodded, he knew how much this annual match meant to his godfather. He had taken part in it for many years, and had ensured that neither side ever had to struggle for players by paying for drinks and bar food in the Snitcher's Head after the match.

'Now, put your bag down, by the deckchair, we've fought hard to ensure no one else pinched it, then go off with Elspeth and wash the dust from your throat.'

It was surprisingly cool inside the pavilion, and Tolstoy noticed a suspicion of musty, mouldy pine in the atmosphere, but there was also a hint of expensive perfume overlying that, a smell that grew stronger the nearer they drew to the bustling kitchen area. Elspeth marched her charge up to the counter and left him there, while she headed into the kitchen, merging with the constantly shifting crowd of mothers, wives, sisters and girlfriends who were toiling over the teams' teas and putting together sandwiches and cakes for the spectators. Some of the faces of the volunteers behind the counter were vaguely familiar to Tolstoy, although putting a name to any of them would be impossible, he knew.

As he waited at the counter Tolstoy turned around and took in the pavilion, somewhere he had not often visited. To his left was the home dressing room, to his right the visitors', while he was in the meeting room, which doubled as a dining room during matches. There were honours boards on the walls where there were no windows, and glass cases containing caps, balls, bails and other fading witnesses to past glories. There were bats too, hanging from the walls, browned and peeling, dented and dusty, relics of an age when makers' names were marks of quality, rather than badges of commerce. Beneath each glass case and bat could be seen a small typewritten label, explaining the significance of the particular artefact and its part in the club's history to any who might be interested.

On the wall above the entrance to the kitchen was a photograph, in a faded sepia tint, of a stern-looking man dressed in Victorian cricket garb, all starched formality and unyielding fabric, and holding a bat, probably one of those on the walls. This imposing figure was Hubert's great-great-grandfather, Willem, who had played for the club in the early nineteenth century, and who had overseen the construction of the pavilion in the 1850s. The old boy had a severe glint about him. Narrow-faced, and probably narrow-minded too, like so many of the Victorian grandees, thought Tolstoy, a little unfairly. But, by all accounts, he had been a fair cricketer in his day. But it had been Hubert's great-great-great-great-grandfather Cornelis, who had founded Stottenden Cricket Club shortly after the turn of the eighteenth century, although in those early days it was known simply as the Manor. Generation after generation of Stottenden inhabitants had since benefited from the de Groots' philanthropy and had been able to enjoy cricket down the centuries.

Tolstoy was still ruminating on what the ground would have looked like around two hundred and fifty years earlier, with no pavilion for starters, when he was pulled from his reverie by the mellow tones of Elspeth. 'Here you are, Tolstoy,' and she placed a pint glass, misted with cold, into his hand. He thanked her and for a few moments concentrated on the sharp lemon freshness as it washed away the summer dryness in his throat and quenched his thirst, adding a soothing chill to his overheated self. He placed the quickly emptied glass onto the counter, pulled out his handkerchief and dabbed delicately at his mouth.

'Would you like a slither of cake?' asked a dark-haired young woman from behind the counter. She was dressed immaculately, petite and possessed of boundless confidence, even when guilty of such an appalling malapropism. Tolstoy debated the worth of correcting her use of a verb describing the motion of a snake, slither, instead of "sliver", a noun denoting a thin slice or splinter of something such as glass or cake. It had irritated him, and more so since she sounded reasonably well-educated, but perhaps not quite as well as she thought she was. He decided that playing the schoolmaster with her, especially in public, might not be a good idea. He bit back the correction, muttering a polite refusal, before following Elspeth back outside.

She guided him back to his godfather. 'Now, sit down,' Elspeth instructed Tolstoy, indicating the vacant deckchair.

Warily, for Tolstoy knew how treacherous this item of furniture could be, he lowered himself onto the striped canvas, all the while dreading what "touchdown" might bring.

His misgivings were not without substance. His backside caught the front edge of the seat, and as the rest of his body looked ready to settle in, so the evil contraption, freed from its locked position by the inadvertent early brush with Tolstoy's buttocks, collapsed, giving the unfortunate young man no chance of recovery, committed as he was to sitting, thus all his weight was in the act of being transferred from legs to the now non-existent seat.

He collapsed, toppling backwards, feet waving frantically in the air, and for a moment, just one brief moment, he resembled nothing so much as a beetle that was struggling to get off its back and onto its feet again.

The immediate audience failed dismally to suppress a titter at Tolstoy's accident. He was covered in embarrassment and shame, the blush suffusing his features even more deeply than the previous one when he had trodden on the young woman's hair.

31

Elspeth came to his rescue, no trace of a smile on her face, only concern for his welfare. 'Darling, are you all right? You haven't hurt yourself, have you?'

He responded with what was meant to be a reassuring denial, but on leaving his mouth it sounded rather more like an irritated grunt. With an effort he raised himself onto his elbows, then, by degrees onto his feet. He restored the deckchair from "flatpack" to seat mode and tried again, applying even more caution than he had shown at his first attempt. This time there were no alarums and, breathing a sigh of relief, he accepted the glass of lemonade which Elspeth had purchased for him after he had demolished the first one. 'It's a good job you weren't holding this glassful,' she said with a gentle smile and Tolstoy nodded his assent.

'All straight, now?' asked his godfather.

'I hope so.'

'Good. Ah!' De Groot was watching the cricket and at that precise moment a wicket fell. 'That could be the end of it now,' he said, shaking his head. 'We are seven down, with just 104 on the board. It's not enough. Oh, wait! I forgot, we have Harry coming in at number nine.'

'Harry?' queried his godson.

'Yes. Harry Stoke, the colonel's gamekeeper. Moved to the village at the beginning of January to take over the shoot for the colonel, but he only recently revealed that he had played a bit of cricket. I have to say, he bats a lot better than most village number nines, in fact better than most village middle order batsmen. Thank goodness I insisted that he played for the Guns, because when he's on song he is quite something with the bat. A real big-hitter. And a left-hander to boot. The thing is, he doesn't play regularly enough, because the shoot occupies so much of his time. Says he doesn't want to let anyone down, so he bats down the order and is ostensibly picked for his bowling, left arm seam.'

De Groot swivelled in his seat to face his wife and their guest. 'Well,' he added, 'we might see a few fireworks shortly, because Harry can certainly hit the ball,' he paused, 'well, except when he misses it of course!'

The new batsman's first shot illustrated perfectly what de Groot had predicted. 'Hah! Harry is not going to let us down,' pronounced Hubert as the noise subsided. 'That's a colossal shot. Six all the way.' He applauded enthusiastically.

Tolstoy, having admired the execution of the shot and the exaggerated follow-through, inquired of his godfather how another member of the Guns XI had fared. 'How did Charlie bat?'

'Very well for seven balls. A couple of boundaries, one a delicious on-drive, then an intemperate heave. A shame really, because he can usually be counted on to weigh in with a decent knock.'

Satisfied that his old schoolfriend Charlie Hornchurch had at least scored a few runs, Tolstoy switched subjects and asked what the latest news on the Buttercup Field campaign might be.

'Ah, well, we had a bit of drama. It must be almost four months ago. Yes, it was back at the beginning of April, and we really thought we had it cracked. Piers St John Worth, one of the village residents, although in fact he lives a little way out of Stottenden. He hasn't been here that long, perhaps three years, certainly no more, anyway, he's something in the City, but in his leisure time he's an amateur botanist. Anyway he had everyone dancing in the pub one evening when he claimed to have found a buttercup in the Buttercup Field. And not just any old buttercup, but apparently a rare one, *ranunculus arvensis* he called it, although its common name is corn buttercup, or scratch bur. Piers said it was the first one to have been found this far south, and the first example in this country for a quarter of a century; the previous one was found in Shropshire. Now that was just what the campaign needed, a rare plant growing in the Buttercup Field, and not just any old rare plant, but a rare buttercup.'

'Good gracious,' exclaimed Tolstoy. 'It must have been some sort of joke. No one has ever seen so much as a petal in the Buttercup Field, let alone a buttercup.'

Hubert smiled: 'I kid you not. He had a photograph of it, which he produced at the bar. Jo, the barmaid – incidentally Elspeth thinks she has a thing for you – rang me and asked me to come over, which I duly did.

'I have to say it was not the clearest of photos, and it was quite difficult to make out anything that remotely resembled a plant let alone a buttercup, and it was just too dark for anyone to be able to see it more clearly in the flesh, as it were. So everyone decided to celebrate anyway, because there was photographic proof, well of the leaves at least, there was no bright yellow flower. In fact, I could not see even a bud. So the Snitcher's Head stayed open until very late that night.

'The following morning we all gathered at the gate to the Buttercup Field and Piers led us in. He took us right to the spot where he had photographed the plant. And sure enough there it was, although, as I say, there was no evidence of a flower, but the leaves were definitely buttercup, Piers

34

showed us a picture in a wildflower book. It was decided to keep an eye on the plant and not tell the council until the thing was in flower, then we would take thousands of photos of it and make a big deal about the Buttercup Field being a site of special scientific interest, and thus we would beat the developers and Jack Bentley.'

Elspeth interjected at this point. 'Since it is nearly the tea interval I think I shall beat the rush and fetch us a tray of tea and sandwiches. Is that all right with you Tolstoy? And you Hubert?'

Both men nodded. Elspeth rose from her deckchair and made her way back to the pavilion. Before any more conversation ensued there was a further interruption as Harry Stoke got hold of the bowling again and hoisted the ball clear over the mid-wicket boundary for another six, a shot which, Tolstoy noted, had helped the batting side's total past the 175 mark. Stoke had also just reached his half century and the Guns' innings was looking far healthier now as they galloped towards two hundred.

'I wonder if Harry'll get to three figures,' Hubert mused.

'How many overs left?'

'Let me see, I think, yes I think eight.'

'Hmm, might be pushing it,' at which point the gamekeeper struck another hefty blow which cleared the rope to more cheers.

'Yes, and anyway he might run out of partners.'

'Not if he can keep the strike, as he appears to be doing,' Tolstoy observed.

A groan from the spectators had godfather and godson focusing on the action. A wicket had fallen. Thankfully, thought Tolstoy, not Harry Stoke, who was by now in the

35

seventies. 'Well,' said his godfather, 'back to the Buttercup Field.' And the pair of them returned to their original conversation.

'Everything was looking fine for the next week or ten days, although there was still no sign of a flower, then we had a hard overnight frost, and the following day the thing we had all feared had happened – the plant had died. Piers was inconsolable. For days he was seen just standing in the Buttercup Field, head bowed as if he was praying for divine help. Finally it was decided to dig up the plant, and try to preserve it as evidence of a sort and suggest that another plant might grow in the spot next year.

'And that is when things took a very interesting twist. Ned Kincaid volunteered to dig up the remains of the *corn* buttercup. Piers said it should be left in the ground, that something might grow from the roots, but Ned reckoned if there was one buttercup plant there, then there would be others. But when he dug into that horrible sticky Kentish clay he struck not more clay, but rather potting compost.'

'Potting compost?' queried Tolstoy. 'In Kentish clay?'

'Quite,' said Hubert. 'It had us all wondering. The committee called Piers to a meeting to quiz him about it. Maybe, as a botanist, we thought, he would know something about soils as well. It was all just informal, although initially Piers refused to make any comment about anything, soil or buttercup, but the committee persisted, indeed almost forcing him to answer their many questions. I mean it was all amicable enough as I say, and indeed I'm told everyone had quite a convivial evening as it happened. So much so that finally Piers caved in and spilled the beans. He confessed to the committee that he had crept into the field in February, with a plant that he had dug up from somewhere else in the country – so there's another offence there, although no one is going to shop him because apart from the village no one else knew about the "rare" buttercup. He admitted he had been stupid, but it was all in a good cause, and he had learned that buttercups do not transplant easily, or at least *ranunculus arvensis* does not transplant that readily. So, anyway, there's a bit of drama for you.'

While Tolstoy was digesting the information about the buttercup plot, both men then turned their attention to the action in the middle, where there was more drama. The timing was unfortunate because local hero Harry Stoke, possibly looking to reach his century in dramatic fashion, heaved across the line at the opposition's oldest team member, a local farm worker who had been bowling the slowest medium pace deliveries for at least half a century. Slow they may have been, but they were always accurate; hit it and the ball would invariably be dismissed to the boundary, miss it and it would be the batsman crossing the boundary rope. And that is precisely what happened to Harry. Ninety-seven not out and going for a big one he suffered the humiliation of having his middle stump knocked backwards very gently and off the players came, the Guns all out for 233, a more than respectable total, which they were confident could be defended. The members of the Beaters team formed a guard of honour to see the gamekeeper off and into the pavilion, which had been emptied of spectators to give both teams a modicum of peace and space, before trooping in behind him to take their places at the dining table for what many considered to be the best moment of the day – tea.

THREE

The tea had been every bit as good as all the previous ones he had enjoyed at Stottenden, thought Tolstoy. Elspeth, refusing his offer of help with the transporting of food and drink, had brought back two huge plates, one piled high with assorted sandwiches and the other groaning with a veritable mountain of cakes. She had then returned to the pavilion for the cups of tea. Consumption was duly completed and, thus sated, relaxed and pleasantly warm, Tolstoy finally gave in to the tiredness that was sweeping over him in waves. Cautiously he leaned back in the deckchair and closed his eyes. The chink of crockery, the clatter of cutlery, the chatter of different conversations around him and the return of the players to the centre of the action faded gradually into the background. He slipped gently into the arms of Morpheus and dozed.

'Warren, darling!' Elspeth de Groot called softly, while simultaneously shaking him very gently. 'Tolstoy, wake up.' His eyelids flickered initially as he slowly returned to consciousness. Finally he opened his eyes. 'Sorry, I must have dozed off.'

He looked up at Elspeth and saw that she had someone with her. A female someone. Tolstoy, ever mindful of his manners, struggled to leave the deckchair, almost over-balancing before achieving verticality. As he drew himself to his full height of 6ft 1in he found himself face to face with the chestnut-haired beauty on whose tresses he had inadvertently trodden on his way around the ground. He blushed again. Considered a further apology. Rejected the idea because of the explanations it would entail to his godfather and Elspeth, and instead stared dumbly at the young woman.

A smiling Elspeth said, 'Tolstoy, may I introduce Henrietta Charles, the daughter of some dear friends.' Tolstoy tentatively proffered his hand as Elspeth explained, 'Henry, this is Warren Pearce, Hubert's godson. Of course, we don't usually call him Warren, because, for obvious reasons, everyone feels his nickname is a lot more fun to use.' As Tolstoy's slightly sweaty hand encountered the cool, smooth surface of Henrietta's right hand for a surprisingly firm shake, he felt himself blushing even more deeply, and he became aware that his heart was beating loudly enough for everyone around to hear.

He muttered, or more correctly, croaked, a lame 'How do you do?' before subsiding into embarrassed silence. Henrietta, for her part, seemed content to let a blanket of disinterest cloak any response from her, and conversation between them consequently stalled before it could really get started.

Elspeth, not one given to unnecessary chitchat, found herself trying to build a conversational bridge between the two. 'We haven't seen Tolstoy in ages, he used to be here most summers, but now, what with work, things seem to get in the way of visits to Kent. Do you get down to Kent regularly, Henry?'

'Mmmm? Oh, sorry, not as much as Mummy and Daddy would like me to, but often enough for me.'

Tolstoy found himself gazing at Henrietta and inhaling her perfume as if it were life-sustaining oxygen. She was stunning. He was smitten.

He was also unable to form any thoughts, let alone words, that might detain Henrietta in conversation for a lifetime or two. What thoughts that did fill his head were hardly suitable for voicing to anyone anywhere at any time. And especially not Henrietta Charles. Certainly not after what he had done with one of his size 13 feet. Elspeth tried again. 'Are you down for the day, or the weekend?'

Henrietta, who had been looking over Tolstoy's left shoulder at someone or something that evidently held a great deal more interest than did this stick-thin dullard standing before her, was slow to reply.

'Um, the weekend,' she said, in a distant voice.

'So's Tolstoy, aren't you, darling?'

He nodded. At that very instant a sentence occurred to him. One that he could direct at Henrietta. First though he had to let the words fall into a semblance of order. Unfortunately, by the time they did, and he had just about engaged voice to brain, Henrietta was announcing, 'Oh, there's someone I simply must speak to. Nice to have met you' [to Tolstoy]. 'Sorry, catch up later' [to Elspeth]. And off she went. Tolstoy followed her progress as she made her way back through the throng of people. She did it so gracefully, he thought. She moved like an athlete, or a dancer, a ballerina. What a contrast, he thought, with himself.

'Are you all right, Tolstoy?' asked Elspeth. 'Only you didn't seem to have very much to say.'

'Sorry, I was still a bit dozy, needed a bit more time to come to,' he said. 'Henrietta seemed very pleasant. She has a lovely voice.'

'Oh she's a super young woman and you're right, she does have a lovely voice. Little wonder that she's a newsreader on the BBC World Service. She reads the news on the main radio news programmes, sometimes she is on in the mornings, other times you hear her in the evenings. She has a truly wonderful voice. It's really mellow. Perfect diction. She enunciates everything so clearly. Her parents are really proud of her. But she's so wrapped up in her career that she's still single. She seems to have no time to herself. I always thought these television and radio people spent their free time partying. Incredibly, her parents have met just two men, whom she has brought down here, in the eight years since she left university. She has probably had other boyfriends up in London, but I can't understand why some man has not snapped her up already. She is perfectly gorgeous to look at and she has a brain as well. It's a pity she didn't stay a little longer just now, I'm sure the two of you would have got along well. Still you are bound to run into her again over the next two days.'

Tolstoy hoped most fervently that he would run into her again, although not literally of course, and this time preferably without inflicting any damage to her. He glanced at the scoreboard and was jolted. 'Good heavens! They've lost six wickets. How long was I asleep for?'

Elspeth smiled. 'About an hour and a half. You were so deeply asleep that I didn't have the heart to wake you, well not until I spotted Henrietta heading in our direction, and then I really had to disturb you, otherwise it would have looked so rude, don't you think, if I had left you snoring gently in the deckchair while carrying on a conversation across your sleeping self?'

Tolstoy nodded his agreement before shaking the same part of his anatomy in wonderment that he had not been woken by the progress of the match, the fall of the wickets or the noise of the crowd. 'Where's Hubert?'

'He's had to go home. He is really not feeling too well. It's his cancer. He is getting noticeably more tired and weaker too, and he seems to be in more pain daily, although he never actually lets on, he is so stoical about it.'

There was a catch in her voice as she added, 'They don't expect him to reach Christmas, which means he will miss our ruby wedding anniversary.'

Tolstoy put an arm around Elspeth's shoulders. He said nothing, because there was nothing he felt he could say. He reflected ruefully that it was the second time in the space of a few minutes that he had been rendered wordless in the company of a woman. And on both occasions, he felt it was his inadequacy, his seeming inability to communicate with the opposite sex, that was the root cause of such reticence.

'Thank you, Tolstoy.' Elspeth eased away from him, composed herself, then sat down alongside him. 'Let's watch the action. Shouldn't be too long now, I would have thought.'

Indeed the Beaters were but a handful of runs away from victory, and barely had he settled back in his deckchair than a chubby batsman executed – *the mot juste for the situation*, thought Tolstoy – an elegant cut and the match was over, the Guns well beaten in the end. As the players left the field Tolstoy and Elspeth got to their feet again, the former then taking it upon himself to fold both chairs and take them over to the side of the pavilion where they were habitually stacked under an awning.

'Will you be going to the pub with everyone?' Elspeth asked.

'Would that be all right with you?' came the response. 'Because if you have anything planned then of course I can give it a miss.'

'No, dear, you go and enjoy yourself. I'll have a light supper prepared for you for when you get in. Perhaps don't be too late, though, because I think Hubert wants a further chat with you about everything.'

'I won't be late,' he promised. Elspeth turned away to speak to someone, while Tolstoy heard himself hailed by someone in the pavilion. With a smile Tolstoy recognised his old school friend, and a popular member of the Guns XI, Charlie Hornchurch, poking his head out of the window of the "Home" dressing room. As Tolstoy approached the pavilion the head addressed him. 'Tolstoy, you old dog! How are things?'

'Charlie, my dear chap! Well. And you?'

'Couldn't be better. Let me finish changing and I'll reveal all.'

The head disappeared and Tolstoy moved around to the front of the pavilion.

He and Charlie had known each other since prep school. The fact that Tolstoy's friend was a fair cricketer, a solid batsman and fine close fielder, whereas Tolstoy was hopeless at cricket and all sport, merely served to bring the two closer. Tolstoy was in part responsible for Charlie's presence in the Guns XI. It was he who had persuaded Charlie to come down to Stottenden with him and stay as a guest of the de Groots a few years earlier. Coincidentally on that weekend the village XI had been a man short and so Charlie, kitted out with borrowed gear, had been roped in to play and made an instant impression with the bat, so much so that the colonel and Hubert de Groot had jointly decided that he would be an ideal addition to their annual cricket match and thus it was that Charlie would spend more than an occasional spring and summer weekend in Stottenden, when he would also turn out for the village cricket team, as well as paying several visits during the shooting season.

While waiting for his friend to reappear, Tolstoy allowed his gaze to sweep around the ground. He still found it hard to believe that one day it would be his, his responsibility. Would he want to change any of it? Not a chance. Would he try to improve the facilities? Possibly, but then again, perhaps not. Perhaps he should consider some form of permanent shelter from rain and relentless sunshine for spectators. But then again... A new score box might not be a bad thing, instead of the scoreboard, have the scorers inside the score box, an electronic one of course, that way they would be sheltered from the extremes of the weather and their scorebooks, more importantly would be spared the occasional soaking. Yes. A score box with room for maybe four people, to allow the scorers a couple of scoreboard operators as well. And four pairs of eyes would result in more accurate records of matches. Right. That was decided, then. He smiled to

44

himself at having a goal. And such a positive one. He would tell his godfather. He hesitated. Maybe not. Perhaps he would look too grasping and vulture-like. Changing things before Hubert had played his final innings. Yes, it might be seen as being a bit insensitive. He would leave it.

He was interrupted in his musings by the sight of the massed waves and curls of Henrietta Charles, in animated conversation with a tall, athletically built man. Her back was to Tolstoy, but he could see, just from the way her head was tilted, and the way she was leaning slightly towards the broad-shouldered man, that this was someone with whom she wanted to have a conversation, in contrast to her second, brief, encounter with Tolstoy. Then the man turned slightly in Tolstoy's direction and he realised that it was Harry Stoke, the gamekeeper and heroic batsman. Well, Tolstoy shrugged mentally, I can't compete with him for Henrietta's interest.

He turned away and focused his attention instead on the entrance to the pavilion, whence he expected to see Charlie emerge any time soon. Out of the corner of his eye he was still aware of Henrietta Charles, her head bobbing enthusiastically at something Harry was saying, but he managed to resist the temptation to turn around fully and gaze at her once more.

He was then distracted by the dark-haired young woman who had earlier offered him a "slither" of cake. 'Hello again. Are you waiting for me?' She had paused on the steps of the pavilion, a quizzical look on her face.

Tolstoy was instantly covered in confusion and blushed deeply. Another near-mute moment in female company for him, and he began to wonder about this particular day and what, or who, might still be lying in wait for him. 'I'm sorry?

Um… I'm waiting for my friend Charlie, who is changing at the moment,' he explained, his tone and look clearly confused and bordering on embarrassment.

She smiled at him. 'It's OK, I was only joking. But you did look a little distracted, lost even, so I thought I'd check, that's all.' She came down the steps. 'That was quite a crescendo to the match. So exciting,' she added, then, without waiting for his response, made to move past him. Tolstoy, for his part, was wondering whether to correct her use of crescendo, when she meant climax, but once again decided against it. He moved aside slightly, although it was not necessary, since there were acres of space around him, and allowed her to ease past him.

However she had only moved a few yards when she stopped, looked over her left shoulder and asked, 'Are you going to the pub?'

'Yes,' a pause, 'with my friend.'

'Good, I'll see you there, then.' And with that she slipped away, Tolstoy's eyes following her trim figure as she trailed after the throng that was heading for the entrance to the field, and thereafter, for the majority no doubt, the Snitcher's Head. She was certainly not unappealing, he thought, lovely blue eyes – he had failed to notice what colour eyes Henrietta Charles had, although he guessed they would be green, given the colour of her hair. After all, that was the traditional combination, red hair with green eyes, wasn't it? Whatever further thoughts he might have had about the colour of Henrietta Charles' eyes, or the trim, young woman were stopped in their tracks by another call to him. 'Warren!' Tolstoy turned and waited for Neville Davis, the vicar of St Martin's, to join him.

'Good afternoon, Neville, did you enjoy the match?'

'Yes, rather exciting I thought. A pity Harry didn't get to three figures, still John Preddy is a wily old fox, his bowling looks so innocuous, so hittable. But more often than not it proves to be missable, as poor Harry found out.'

'Yes. He's earned the title "The Sly Slow Bowler" all right,' agreed Tolstoy. 'How come you weren't playing for the Guns today? They could have done with a bit of your Caribbean clubbing. I saw your century earlier this season for the Village XI against Comenden, it was something to behold. How many balls was it? Sixty-eight? Shades of the legendary Sir Vivian Richards. Don't tell me you were dropped for Harry Stoke?'

The priest smiled at Tolstoy. 'No, I wasn't dropped. Out injured.' And he held up his right hand. 'I broke a bone when I tripped in the churchyard the other day, so for the next six weeks or so I am sidelined. Enough of me, did I see you chatting up Kate Harborne a moment ago? Nice woman.'

'Is that her name? The dark-haired woman? Kate Harborne?'

'Yes. She runs a gift shop in Tunbridge Wells. Quite successful, too, I'm told. Although she used to have quite a high-powered job working in a museum. She's a historian, and I believe she used to specialise in old manuscripts, or some such. Nice woman.'

'I was most certainly not chatting her up,' Tolstoy mustered some indignation into his voice. 'It was more a case of her chatting to me. Said she'd see me in the pub. I'll certainly be there, for a short while at least, but not because of her. I'm taking my old school friend Charlie Hornchurch, who captained the Guns today, to the Squealer's for a couple of catch-up pints.'

'Have you heard about all the fuss over the Buttercup Field?'

'Yes, Hubert has been telling me. But it sounds as if it is all going to end happily ever after.'

'I wouldn't be too sure. A lot will depend on how the public hearing goes. There are those in the village who say that the government is very keen to push through developments such as the one being proposed by Jack Bentley. And it can't be denied, we could do with more housing in the area, and maybe even the village. Yet somehow I wouldn't like to see the Buttercup Field sprouting houses. It would be better if Jack Bentley sold one of his fields, perhaps on the outskirts of Stottenden, for residential development.'

Tolstoy nodded his agreement, just as a hearty slap jolted him. His closest friend, the nearest he had to a brother, had stolen up behind him and announced his arrival in typical fashion. Charlie Hornchurch was a trifle shorter than Tolstoy, a trifle wider and a trifle heavier. He was also a trifle less serious than his old school friend. But then, reflected Tolstoy, he could afford to take life and himself less seriously, since he had none of the material worries of lesser mortals. As next-in-line to the fifteenth Baron of Upminster, whose wealth was vested in businesses and property in the south of Essex, but whose 1,000-acre family seat lay in the north of the county, nudging against the boundary with Suffolk, Charlie Hornchurch stood to inherit untold riches should he outlive the incumbent, his older brother, Algy, twenty-five years his senior, and childless. As it was, Charlie managed a more modest estate a few miles from the family seat as well as working in the City.

'What ho, Rev! Enjoy the match?'

'Yes, I was just telling Warren, it was rather good in parts. And it might have been a bit closer had Harry Stoke not been done by old John Preddy, who must bowl the slowest ball in England, but he gets more than his share of wickets for all his lack of pace. Right, must slip away, got to put the finishing touches to tomorrow's sermon. Bye.'

Charlie Hornchurch turned to his friend. 'Now, Tolstoy, why so glum? It's only a game after all.' Hornchurch dropped a large leather holdall containing his kit and bats at his feet, in readiness for a goodish chat.

'I'm not glum,' insisted Tolstoy. 'I was merely lost in thought momentarily.'

'Really? You could have fooled me, old son. You look like the crow who lost his piece of cheese thanks to the flattering comments of the hungry fox. And if it wasn't the result of what was an exciting match, then what is it that has left you so pensive?'

Tolstoy opened his mouth to reply but was beaten to speech by a figure that loomed into view on his left. 'Excuse me, sorry to butt in like this.' The interruptor was a large man, in his late sixties or early seventies, it was difficult to tell. 'Warren, how are you?'

It was the colonel. 'Good afternoon Andrew, very well thank you. You seem to have made a rather good signing for the Guns this year. Your keeper can certainly hit a cricket ball.'

'Yes, in fact,' he turned to Charlie, 'not since your debut has a newcomer made such an impression on the team or on a match.'

The modest Charlie demurred, 'I don't recall ever making such an explosive contribution to a game. And my best innings is a shade over fifty, so I think Mr Stoke has the potential to make a far greater impression on this match, and on the village XI than I could ever hope to do. He really can hit the ball. Surely he should be batting up the order?'

'We discussed that, but he felt that until he is more established here, and he is still trying to sort out the shoot for me, it would be better all round if he came in to lift the tail, so to speak.'

'He certainly did that,' said a smiling Tolstoy. 'Now, a change of subject,' said the colonel. 'I wondered if you were intending going to the Snitcher's Head in the next few minutes, because if you are I am trying to get a few of us together to discuss tactics over the Buttercup Field.'

'Yes, Charlie and I are about to make our way over there. Where though? It's going to be heaving. Back bar?'

'Yes, Nick Marten has promised to keep everyone else out of there until the committee has finished its business, which shouldn't take too long. Right, see you there, Warren. Pleasure to see you again, Charlie.' The colonel wheeled around and strode off in the general direction of the pub.

'He's such a gentleman,' said Charlie.

'Yes, he is. He's been extremely active in the campaign to save the Buttercup Field. Have you been following events?' A shake of the head from Charlie prompted Tolstoy to give his friend a brief run-down.

After which he asked, 'By the way, where are you staying? Did you take my advice and book yourself into the Star and Eagle in Goudhurst?'

'Absolutely. Good beer, great food and a lively crowd. An excellent recommendation, so thanks for that. A good runner-up to the Snitcher's Head as well. Anyway, what were we saying before Andrew came along? Ah yes, I was accusing you of resembling a hungry crow that had lost its piece of cheese. You appeared to be about to explain everything, so I am all ears once more, my dear chum.'

Tolstoy hesitated, then, 'Hubert has deteriorated, which is depressing enough; he has always been there, but now he tells me time is running out. Then this afternoon he had to leave the match, wasn't there for the finale, which is unheard of. And although she has seemed OK, Elspeth momentarily lost it today, and after he had left she told me that Hubert has been in a lot of pain of late and is not expected to make it to Christmas. She is extremely distressed. Normally she is not one for overt displays of emotion, but she let her guard drop after Hubert did the unthinkable and left this, his favourite cricket match, before it was halfway through and returned to the house because of the pain he was in.'

'I'm so sorry, Tolstoy. I had no idea. I mean, I knew he was unwell, hence me booking in to the Star and Eagle, but I had not realised that things were quite that bad. I didn't manage to get to see him before the start of proceedings today, but fully intend to see him tomorrow at the Manor.

'Well, here's me, full of the joys of summer, and bursting with news of a job offer, and I ignore your obvious sadness, treating it far too lightly. Can you forgive an old friend?'

'There's nothing to forgive, Charlie. Hubert is very old. Far older than that even. An end awaits us all. I am over-reacting. It was just the way I found out.'

'What do you mean?'

'Well, by way of introducing his impending end, Hubert announced out of the blue, this was back in November, that I am to inherit Stottenden Manor and all the land, which includes this cricket ground. Forget Harry Stoke and his batting, this news knocked *me* for six, I can tell you. I would have told you sooner, but at the time he swore me to secrecy. This was just between Elspeth, him and me.'

'Good grief! Welcome to the club!'

Tolstoy smiled wryly. 'I hardly think ownership, inherited ownership at that, entitles me to join you and your country landowners' set. For a start I have no wish to belong to such a club, with the greatest respect to you; furthermore, I have no title to bring with me, and therefore could not qualify. I'd be black-balled unanimously. For which, many thanks.'

'Well, be that as it may, you are still to be congratulated. There's real history here at Stottenden Manor. And not just the cricket club either. I'm not exactly envious, but I have to admit, to take over ownership of a cricket ground and become the custodian of its club's history is a signal honour.' Tolstoy, feeling something akin to a lump growing in his throat, merely nodded, aware, at the same time, of a moistening of an eye or two, but, too manful to bring up a finger to aid with the dispersal of said moisture, he bore the indignity, if that is what it was, with stoicism.

Charlie continued, 'And whether you want to belong to "the club" or not, you can still turn to me for advice on the pitfalls and pratfalls of land ownership at any time, once you take over, that is.'

All this time the two friends had been standing in front of the pavilion, and both became aware that they were pretty much the last people in the cricket field, apart from a group of women and a couple of young boys clearing things up, collecting litter and carting dirty crockery to the pavilion for washing.

'I think you have something to celebrate,' said Charlie. 'And as it happens, so do I, an offer of a new job with a rival hedge fund. Lots more dosh. Lots more responsibility. I have accepted and start in two weeks' time. So, with two such pieces of good news there is no finer place for celebration in this county than the old Snitcher's Head. I think we should depart promptly for the bar and once there raise a glass or three of the Snitcher's splendid Fuggles ale to our good news, notwithstanding the sad news about your godfather.'

'What about your car? Did you park on the ground?'

'No, I had a word with Nick Marten and he kindly allowed me to park in the pub car park. So let's go and have a drink.'

Tolstoy grinned. 'Let me buy the first round.' Together they strolled across the outfield, enjoying their surroundings and admiring the charm of the cricket ground in the evening sunshine, while anticipating a pleasurable session in the old pub.

FOUR

Most of the spectators and players were outside the Snitcher's Head – their cars lining the narrow road, a parade of pecuniary power – when Tolstoy and Charlie rolled up, at least that's how it appeared to them. Tolstoy thought that at least the bar would be negotiable. How wrong could a chap be? There was barely room enough for one body, let alone two, inside. The public bar was heaving with thirsty bodies and bulging wallets. The clamour, laughter and hubbub was mind-numbing, thought Tolstoy as he eased and squeezed his way around and through groups of tightly-packed drinkers. It took a couple of minutes to reach the bar, which seemed to be under siege from a forest of waving arms, and on the way there Tolstoy inadvertently caught the eye of the dark-haired woman, Kate, what was her name? She gave him a dazzling smile, but that lost its lustre almost immediately when, over her shoulder, Tolstoy caught a glimpse of a mane of glossy chestnut hair, and he found himself thinking of sultry-voiced Henrietta Charles. Once at the bar an incredulous Tolstoy was served almost straightaway by the efficient Jo, who also gave him a dazzling smile. On returning to Charlie, who had sensibly hung back on the fringe of the human barrier, Tolstoy reminded his old friend that he had to pop into the back bar for a meeting of the campaign committee.

'No problem. I want to have a quick word with Stoke, the gamekeeper. That was a brilliant innings, and he also took a wicket with his half-decent left arm medium pacers. He will be one hell of an asset to the village team over the next few seasons. And of course his place in next year's Guns XI is already assured.'

'Right oh, see you in a while,' and Tolstoy edged his way towards the back bar. He slipped into the relative peace of the smaller room. There were already half a dozen or so people sitting around two tables that had been pulled together.

Tolstoy recognised a couple of them. Andrew Barcombe was naturally there and as chairman of the committee had unsurprisingly seated himself at the head of the tables. He had to be in his seventies, but Tolstoy knew he was as sharp as a tack, and, as an ex-SAS colonel, he had proved to be a formidable leader of Stottenden's fight, well-versed in the logistical side of things as well as the management of committees. Then there was Kate – what *was* her name? – Harborne! Yes, that was it. And he had to admit to himself that he was beginning to find her presence rather welcome. She indicated an empty chair beside her, so he moved around to the far side of the tables and joined her.

'Hello, I didn't realise you were on the committee,' said Tolstoy.

'I wasn't originally, but because I live in the village and I am passionate about everything to do with it, including preserving it and its traditions, it seemed like a good idea. It helps that I have typing and shorthand skills – I spent my gap year learning shorthand and typing before going up to Leeds University to study for a degree in History of Art. I then got a job with a specialist museum in North London, where I used to examine and look after documents and stuff like that. 'Then a while back I decided on a complete change of tack and struck out on my own. I hated the commuting to London and wanted to be my own boss – I was persuaded to come on board the committee in April. This is only about my third meeting.' She paused and blushed. 'I'm so sorry, I didn't mean to pour out my CV like that. How rude of me.' Tolstoy smiled and waved a dismissive hand as she continued, 'How about you? What brings you onto the committee?'

'Well I'm sort of on the committee, but co-opted rather than being a full member. Living in London and occasionally working Saturdays means I can't always get down here for meetings, so rather than be an unreliable, non-attendee, everyone agreed that I just turn up when I can. And I only just learned of this meeting about fifteen minutes ago.'

'I think that's because the colonel has only just had some news himself.'

Tolstoy glanced around at the handful of other people in the room. Nick Marten, the landlord of the Snitcher's Head, he recognised and James Appyltoft, a solicitor, he also knew, although only to say 'Hello' to when spotting him in the bar of the pub. The other two people, a man and a woman, Tolstoy did not know.

They were swiftly identified for him by the colonel, who called the meeting to order and followed it up with introductions. The woman, an elegant blonde of indeterminate age, was Angela Smeaton, a barrister. On her left, a man with short fair hair and a stern expression, was Angela's husband Robert Smeaton, a solicitor in the City, and Kate then whispered in his ear that he was known by everyone as Bertie because of his love of the PG Wodehouse character Bertie Wooster. On Angela's right was a bearded man closer to sixty than fifty. He was Piers St John Worth, who had been described by Hubert de Groot as something in the world of finance, but of more relevance was the fact that he was the amateur botanist who had tried to transplant a rare buttercup in the field. The Reverend Davis had apparently begged off to sort out the following day's sermon.

The colonel called the meeting to order. 'Good evening everyone, thank you for coming here at such short notice. I have received notification that our hearing to establish that the Buttercup Field has fulfilled the role of village green will take place in four weeks' time, on Monday ninth and Tuesday tenth of next month, and it will be held in the village hall. The hours are 10–4pm and it is not expected to run for longer than two days. Indeed, the letter stated that it would not run any longer than that. Now firstly, the letter stated that Jack Bentley has employed a barrister to put his case and we have been advised to do the same, so I wondered, Angela, if your busy schedule might even so allow you to fulfil that role for us? A number of us have agreed to underwrite your fee and your expenses, to try to compensate in part for any financial loss you might sustain during the hearing.' His pause was as good as any question mark, with his raised eyebrows providing the curve.

Angela Smeaton took a moment, then peering over her half-moon spectacles pronounced, 'I shall have to consult my diary, but I have a feeling I shall be free on at least one of those days, if not both. And we have an extremely able junior barrister in our set who could either stand in for me, or in fact take the case, and I can state here and now that the case will be on a *pro bono* basis, no fee. No money will change hands. If I am unable to make it, then I shall pay any and all expenses for the junior's travel, accommodation and incidentals; there is no need for a pooling of resources to cover the costs. After all, this is my village too, and Stottenden's problems are my problems as well as everyone else's. This is an opportunity for me to show willing and actually do something concrete for the cause. So count me in, and I shall ensure that we prepare a comprehensive brief. Mr Bentley's counsel is going to have a fight on his hands.'

Everyone else around the tables broke into a round of applause, before the colonel responded, 'That is extremely generous of you, Angela. I am pretty sure, with your expertise and guidance we will be able to build a fairly convincing case. Now the other thing the letter from the office of Her Majesty's Inspector pointed out was that if any of us wish to question any witness, then we have to register at the outset, giving our name and address etc.

'I think this is most important, and we must make sure that everyone on the committee puts their name forward. We can probably work out a few questions that can be put as well.' He glanced over at Angela Smeaton with a quizzical look.

She stepped in straightaway. 'There will be no need to think of any questions beforehand, and since I, or my junior colleague, will be representing you, there should be no need for anyone else to put questions to the opposition; that will be my role. I shall of course be calling all of you and anyone else in the village as witnesses for our side of things, so if during the course of the hearing something occurs to you, or you think there has been a contradiction in an opposition witness's statement on the stand, then you can let me know by passing me a note. Then, when I call you to the stand, we should be able to address all such points. Quite often, at hearings such as this, a witness will make a claim, perhaps slightly exaggerated, in an attempt to strengthen their case; then later witnesses have been known to state the opposite, or at least to knock down their previous statement, and it is at moments such as that that I shall endeavour to do my job and tear their claims to bits.' She paused and smiled, revealing near-perfect teeth, before sitting back in her chair, leaving the floor to the colonel.

'Well, thank you, Angela, that was very helpful and clear. I think as a committee we must contact everyone in the village and check with them to see if they would be prepared to be called as a witness, always assuming that they would have something relevant to say. There is no point people just volunteering to be a witness if they cannot add something telling to our case, something that might even sway the verdict of the inspector.'

Angela concurred. 'That is a very sensible point, Andrew. Perhaps it would be an idea to set aside an evening when we, as the committee, can get together and interview potential witnesses, a sort of weeding-out process. There may be people who will be repeating what another witness has to say. What we need is ammunition, different points that reinforce our case. Making the same point to the inspector will not persuade him or move him one iota; rather, I fear, it will irritate him and might even count against us when he goes away to weigh up everything.'

The colonel looked happy. 'Excellent idea. We need to find a date when the hall is free between now and the commencement of the hearing, and publicise it, tell family and friends, neighbours and nodding acquaintances that it is imperative they turn up on the evening we decide on and, even if they do not want to be a witness, they might still have something relevant to add to the case, some point that Angela might find useful in the course of the process. So I think, Kate, may we put you in charge of establishing and booking a date for this meeting in the village hall? On reflection I think it has to be in the coming week, so that we, and Angela especially, have time to collate information and prepare witnesses, etc. Can you sort that for us?'

Kate promised to get on with it, and agreed to email everyone once it had been fixed, at which point the colonel declared the meeting closed, and the bar open.

As Tolstoy stood to rejoin Charlie in the main bar the colonel looked up and asked, 'Warren, could you give me a couple of minutes?'

'Of course, Andrew,' and Tolstoy resumed his seat, while the rest of the committee headed out into the crush.

With the back bar emptied the colonel began. 'Firstly I was so sorry to hear of Hubert's situation. While I know he is a hell of an age, he moves like a man thirty years younger. He has always been so active in and around the village and taken a keen interest in its goings-on, from the mundane to the more dramatic, such as the Buttercup Field. He has invariably provided some sort of practical contribution whenever he has been able to. I know he is your godfather, and that you and he are very close, so I wanted to let you know that you have my deepest sympathies for this very sad news.

'But Hubert also told me that you are to take over the house and land, and most importantly, the cricket field, and I applaud him for that. I don't think Stottenden Manor could have been placed in safer hands.'

Tolstoy found himself quite moved. The colonel was not one to wax emotional, so this was quite a statement from him. 'Thank you, Andrew, those are extremely kind words. And I can assure you that when I eventually take over – and Elspeth will continue to live in Stottenden Manor, I shall remain a visitor, although perhaps a more regular one once the situation changes – I shall continue to run things as Hubert is doing. I see no reason for change. Although it did surprise me when I learned, despite what I had always assumed, that the Buttercup Field does not belong to the Manor, nor has it ever. And it would be wonderful were Hubert or Elspeth to unearth a document proving conclusively that it has always been part of the grounds. Never mind, that is probably just pie in the sky.'

The colonel pushed back his chair and got to his feet. Tolstoy followed. 'Now one more thing, Warren. I think if you could make it to this witness meeting later this coming week it would be useful. I feel, given your situation, that you should be a witness, making a good case for access to the cricket field, for one thing. Would you be able to do that?'

'I shall give it some thought, Andrew, but I can't promise anything. I know that from Wednesday on I shall be in Manchester for a series of meetings with an important potential new client company, and we have to prepare for that meeting, but I will do my best. If Angela thinks I could contribute something to our side of things then I will be perfectly happy to appear as a witness, and on Monday I shall book those two days as holiday.'

The pair of them headed for the bar. Thankfully the crowd had thinned, many people spilling out onto the pavement or into the pub garden. Charlie Hornchurch was deep in conversation with Harry Stoke, and, not wanting to interrupt their flow, Tolstoy decided on a top-up of his pint and offered the colonel a drink as well.

'Dry white wine would be perfect,' came the response. As ever Jo served him pretty much the second he reached the bar.

'Fuggles?' she asked.

'Oh, yes please, Jo, and a dry white wine for the colonel, a large one.' He paused, then added, 'And one for yourself?'

With a charming blush Jo said, 'Oh Warren, that is very kind of you. I'll have a small white wine, although I'll save it for later, we aren't allowed to drink while on duty.'

Tolstoy could not help but notice how attractive Jo was. He did enjoy the smile she gave him every time he spoke to her. Physically she appeared to have all the attributes and maybe more. She was fairly tall, and on this occasion was wearing a pair of shorts, very short shorts which amplified the length of her legs, especially, as now, when she was bending over to reach inside the fridge for the bottle of house dry white. He was jolted out of his observations by a question. 'Are you buying? If so, mine's a dry white wine.'

It was Kate Thingummy, who had materialised at his left elbow. Her lack of inches had allowed her to slip up close, under his radar, and his elbow, without him noticing. He half-turned to acknowledge the question, then smiled. 'Oh, OK.' Back to Jo, 'Could you make that another dry white… um, another large one.'

'Sure,' Jo smiled, looking past him at Kate. 'Hello Kate, is this one for you?'

'Yes, it is.'

'Ice with it?'

'No, not this time,' said a clearly embarrassed Kate.

'Do you put ice in your wine?'

'Just occasionally. I like my white wine really cold on hot days like today, and as it melts it makes the wine go further, diluting it, so I don't get too drunk, too quickly.' It seemed to Tolstoy that a certain frostiness had entered her voice. With a view to finding slightly warmer climes he picked up the colonel's wine, spotted him over by the back bar and took the glass over to him, before returning to pay for the drinks.

He established from Jo how much he owed then handed over the cash. Jo gave him another of her generous smiles and said if he was still around when her shift ended she would raise her glass to him. Kate was still standing on his left, not quite leaning on the bar, possibly because she was fairly short, although fairly trim as well. On seeing that Charlie was still chatting to Harry Stoke, Tolstoy steered Kate over to a table near the entrance and pulled out a chair for her.

'What a gentleman,' she said and sat down. He followed, seating himself opposite her.

'Are you eating here tonight?' asked Kate.

'No. Very shortly I am heading over to the Manor for a meal with Elspeth and Hubert.'

'Will you be coming back over after that?'

'Not sure. Depends on what time we finish eating and talking, although I do know Hubert is feeling very tired so he might head to bed early and Elspeth would then almost certainly follow him, so I could well return. I want to talk to Charlie at some point anyway. Catch him before he goes back to the Star and Eagle. I have a feeling he is eating there this evening. What about you? What are you going to do?'

She sipped her wine then said, 'I'll probably eat here and then hang around for a while.'

As she answered him Tolstoy saw that Charlie and Harry had been joined by Henrietta Charles. Lucky old Charlie, thought Tolstoy, getting that close to Miss Charles. He wasn't close for long though. Within seconds of her turning a twosome into a threesome, Charlie was moving away from the other two. He did not seem too disappointed, but he caught Tolstoy's eye, indicating that they should talk and so, remembering his manners, Tolstoy focused on Kate and said, 'Well then, I might very well see you later. Unfortunately, I have to leave you now, because Charlie is finally free of Harry and I do need to have a word, before I head in for dinner. I hope you don't mind.'

'Not at all. May see you later. And thanks for the drink.' She raised her glass to him as he stood and left the table.

Tolstoy had just about drained his glass. Charlie was holding an empty glass as well, so they converged on the bar, ordered two more pints, with Charlie doing the paying this time around. Once again Jo was in immediate attendance and

Tolstoy quickly became aware that she was looking at him all the time she was pulling the pints, smiling at him from time to time. After Charlie had paid, the two friends moved off towards a relatively clear area near the entrance to the garden.

'I reckon that barmaid – Jo isn't it? – has a soft spot for you.'

'I don't think so,' said Tolstoy, feeling a flush stealing across his face. 'I'm no muscled hunk, no sporting Adonis. Anyway, what makes you say that?'

'Just the way she couldn't seem to take her eyes off you when she was pulling our pints. And the way she smiled at you while serving us. She never once looked in my direction. Nice-looking woman, it has to be said.'

'I don't think I'm her type,' Tolstoy blustered. 'Anyway, what happened to you, one second you were in deep conversation with Harry Stoke, the next thing Henrietta Charles joins you and you are off, like a whipped dog.'

'The thing is, when she joined us she barely glanced at me, turned all her charms on Harry, poor bloke, and effectively asked me to leave by saying that she wanted to ask Harry something, and did I mind? I didn't and left them to it. She is a real looker though, don't you agree?'

'Yes, she is, although again I am probably not her type.'

'Are you the type that appeals to that dark-haired stunner with whom you sat for about three minutes just now?'

'Not sure. She seems OK, although her English is not great. She thinks a slither is a sliver, when it's not, and she doesn't know which, of crescendo and climax, comes first.'

'What is a slither, then?'

Tolstoy explained, prompting Charlie to say, 'You are a clever bugger. I haven't got a clue about stuff like that. But of course I remember from school, you read a lot, don't you? I mean I can't imagine you without a book somewhere on your person. In fact, I'll bet there's a book in one of your jacket pockets.'

Tolstoy gave a sheepish smile and lifted the left-hand side of his jacket to reveal the outline of a book in the Harris Tweed. With a sudden flash of insight Charlie said, 'I bet you didn't correct her when she said "slither", nor when she got confused over crescendo and climax. By the way, which does come first?'

Tolstoy shrugged. 'Didn't seem much point in correcting her either time, it would have just embarrassed her.'

'Oh, I see, playing the "parfit, genteel knight" were we?' He paused to grin at his now blushing friend, then continued, 'Perhaps you'll get your opportunity to correct her in private sometime soon. Anyway, I must away. Dinner beckons and I am famished.'

'I'm off too. Elspeth has prepared a meal and I promised her I wouldn't be late. The deadline approaches.'

'I plan to drop round to see Hubert and Elspeth tomorrow morning, late-ish. So I will see you then, and afterwards we could slip over here for a quick pint and a chat before heading off,' said Charlie. Tolstoy agreed, and, after draining their glasses, they stood up and made their way out of the pub, Charlie heading for the car park, Tolstoy crossing the road and walking the short distance to the pillared gateway and the curving drive that led to Stottenden Manor.

Once there he made his way to his room, and after a quick wash and brush-up he headed down the wide staircase to the hall, thence into the kitchen, from which emanated the clatter of food preparation. Elspeth turned as he came through the door. 'Oh Tolstoy, there you are. Perfect timing, I'm just getting things ready for serving. It's a homemade chicken pie, with salad and new potatoes from the garden. And I'm sorry but Hubert is just too exhausted to join us, so you'll have to put up with me. Hubert did say he would try to join us later, but he is in quite a lot of pain and is also feeling dreadfully nauseous, so I wouldn't count on that.'

She began slicing the pie and serving it. 'Tolstoy, would you mind fetching some wine from the cellar, please? A red for me, maybe a Rhone, and whatever you feel like.'

Tolstoy made for a solid-looking oak door to the left of the kitchen entrance, hit the light switch which was on one side, then turned the large iron handle and descended the wide, worn stone steps, his nostrils assailed by the all-pervasive damp, musty smell of the cellar, before stepping into a veritable Aladdin's cave of all things vinous. This first section of the cellar held Hubert's vast collection of wine. In his day, Hubert had been something of a wine buff and over the years had amassed an impressive collection, dominated by French wines, but also featuring Italian, Spanish, New Zealand, Australian, German, Portuguese, South African and even some South American. His godfather had guided and encouraged Tolstoy to follow him in his interest and he now strolled slowly down the rows of brick and cement bins, the racks on the walls and the cases stacked on shelves and on pallets on the floor. Hubert was meticulous in his record-keeping; every bin, rack and case carried a clearly printed manifest of what was there. After a couple of minutes' perusing Tolstoy finally settled on a St Joseph from the Northern Rhone for Elspeth, and after studying the white section, plumped for a Picpoul de Pinet, a refreshing white, which he could never tire of, even though some of his more discerning wine-loving friends were rather dismissive of the product of the South of France.

Returning to the kitchen he found Elspeth laying two places at the large farmhouse table that occupied the centre of the room. He opened the bottles and poured each of them a generous glass, then, at Elspeth's prompting, took his seat. She passed him a plate with a sizeable wedge of chicken pie and told him to help himself to salad and potatoes.

Conversation during the meal was easy, punctuated with comfortable pauses as a mouthful of food or a sip of wine intervened. Finally, plate empty, stomach pleasantly full, Tolstoy sat back in his chair, content. At which point he felt duty bound to broach the subject of his godfather's health.

Elspeth looked at him sadly and said, 'I feel so helpless. He has always been such a vigorous man, physically and mentally. Now, over the last few months he has declined alarmingly. He always seems to be so tired and so weak. I was amazed when he declared that he was going to watch the match today. That is the furthest he has ventured in two months. I wasn't surprised that he failed to stay until the end, but at least he was able to see most of it.'

They soon moved off the subject of Hubert and instead looked back at the cricket match, Elspeth reminding Tolstoy of the meeting with Henrietta Charles. But this subject proved a bit of a downer for Tolstoy as well, and so eventually the conversation, perforce somewhat dilatory and depressing, gradually wound down to very little. Tolstoy found himself yawning. For no apparent reason he felt completely drained. He decided he would forego the late drink at the Snitcher's Head. Elspeth tried to persuade him to head off for bed right then, but he insisted on helping her with the washing-up. That done, he finally said goodnight, and dragged himself upstairs, his mind on the following day and his return to London. He decided on a change of plan. His original intention had been to head home in the afternoon; now he felt he would be better advised leaving in the morning. He was sure his godfather and Elspeth wouldn't mind. And he could ask them to pass on his apologies to Charlie Hornchurch, who would have been expecting to see Tolstoy the following morning when he dropped in at the Manor. He then got into bed and gave himself up to the welcome oblivion of sleep.

FIVE

The bell of St Martin's church tolled dolefully, the sound seeming to merge with the misty rain that partially shrouded the church tower, and adding a soundtrack to what was a mournful and grey day. As he entered the church with Elspeth on his arm, Warren Pearce was astonished at the sight that greeted them. There did not appear to be an empty pew. The whole village and more must be here, thought Tolstoy, as he moved slowly and solemnly up the aisle. Elspeth had not wanted to follow her husband's coffin, preferring instead to precede it by a couple of minutes.

They eventually arrived at the front of the church and Tolstoy stepped to one side to allow Elspeth to slip into her seat. He followed her in, sat down and contemplated the last three months.

His godfather Hubert de Groot had lost his battle with cancer some two months after the cricket match, which, as it turned out, had also been Tolstoy's last visit to Stottenden. While the end had been expected, it was still shocking to Tolstoy. He had immediately taken time off work to come down to provide comfort and help to Elspeth. The administrative tasks following a death were innumerable. There just seemed to be no time for grieving. Tolstoy had been feeling a little guilty that he had not visited Hubert since the cricket match. He had intended to, but his circumstances at work and Hubert's rapidly declining health had dictated otherwise.

The simple service was mercifully brief – one hymn, a psalm, some prayers and a gentle eulogy from one of Hubert's oldest friends – then out to the churchyard for the burial. More prayers, and finally it was all over and the members of the congregation made their way to the Snitcher's Head for the funeral breakfast. Elspeth seemed to be on autopilot, accepting handshakes here, hugs there and the occasional chaste kiss on the cheek, and all the while Tolstoy remained dutifully at her side, accepting the many condolences. It was, as he confessed later to Elspeth, all rather emotionally draining. They had left the breakfast as early as they could and now sat together in the drawing room of the Manor, taking stock, as she put it. She shared a couple of memories of Hubert with Tolstoy, then spoke of her happy marriage to the man, before wondering how she was going to cope with all the day-to-day things that, for the time being, now fell to her to do. 'I hope I'll be able to cope. I don't even know where to look for anything,' she said.

'I'm sure that won't be a problem,' Tolstoy ventured. 'Hubert was an extremely well-organised person, someone of a tidy nature. I'm certain he will have left everything easy for you find, and the chances are that he will have left clear instructions for you on how to pay this or that bill. And anyway, I'll help you.'

'But you have to go to work,' she protested, before adding, 'Do you know something? I have no idea what you do for a living.'

'Well, it's an archive of newspaper and magazine articles and it is also combined with a picture/photographic archive. I am really just a glorified librarian. I look up and copy people's requests for this cutting, article, or that photo and send them to the people. The secretary then sends out an invoice for each request a day or so later and makes sure everyone pays up. Darren, the archivist, collects the articles and cuttings and adds them to the company's computerised archive. We don't just use on-line media sources, we collect hard copy and we have also negotiated to collect printed material and photographs that date from the nineteenth century. And as for time off, that's all been sorted. I'm taking a fortnight off, mostly unpaid, although they do owe me loads of overtime. I'm forever getting calls from the office outside my normal hours, which invariably entail me having to go into the office to find this or that file or photo.' As Elspeth started to interject, Tolstoy hurried on, 'Don't worry. I can afford it. These last couple of months in particular have been manic for me, so I deserve a break. I hope it will show them just how much they rely on me and my goodwill.'

'You are a darling, Tolstoy,' said Elspeth, who was finally coming around to using his nickname. 'I should be most grateful for any help you can give. The first thing that we have to do is to meet the solicitor. I had pencilled in tomorrow for the trip into Tonbridge.'

'Is this for the reading of the will?'

'Yes, although it is pretty much a formality. We are the sole beneficiaries and there are no obvious problems arising from it. That was why I didn't insist on an earlier reading, because knowing that you are invariably very busy on weekdays, and with the solicitor's offices being shut at the weekend, the most convenient time had to be around the funeral, which, by the way, I thought went very well.'

'Yes, it did. A good service. Long enough to do Hubert justice, short enough not to leave people desperate for it to end.'

'Now, before we get too far along the road, I think we need to lay down a few ground rules for when you move in here permanently,' said Elspeth. 'Since I have spent my life cooking for Hubert, I have no problem about cooking for you. Occasionally, however, I might have the odd evening out with friends and so I hope you would be happy fending for yourself.'

She paused and Tolstoy took his cue. 'That's fine by me. I have to confess I am no cook, so if you are not around I will almost certainly slip over the road to the Snitcher's Head for a pub meal.'

'Good, and thank you. I think it might be sensible to set up some kind of kitty for food, and indeed housekeeping. I have a lady who comes in three times a week to help with vacuuming and ironing, so I think we ought to share her cost, if that's all right with you.' Tolstoy nodded. 'And occasionally I have friends around here, the book group for example, and also we have a little bridge party from time to time. Again it would probably be better if you fended for yourself on those occasions, unless you play bridge?' She raised an eyebrow in an inquiring way.

'No, sadly I don't, although I think I might like to learn at some point in the not too distant future,' said Tolstoy.

'Are you much of a television watcher?'

'No, well I mainly watch the news and the odd current affairs programme, but if I can't get access to a television it is not the end of the world. I actually prefer reading.'

'So do I, although, like you, I like to keep up to date with national and international news. I listen to the radio a fair bit as well. Do you like classical music?'

'Yes I do. Rather a lot actually, although I don't play a musical instrument, but yes I enjoy listening to classical music radio stations and I have a fairly large collection of music on various laptops and phones.'

'Well, this is all beginning to sound good. I think we are going to get on rather well,' Elspeth smiled at him. 'But I will say that I do not expect you to spend every evening in with me, or indeed every weekend. If you have somewhere else to go then go. Right,' Elspeth leaned back in her chair, 'that all seems very satisfactory. I shall work out how much kitty we each need to pay in, and then we will see how well it covers our needs. We might even experiment with the two weeks that you are here.'

'That sounds like a good idea,' said Tolstoy. 'By the way, sorry to change the subject but while I think about it, has a new date been set for the Buttercup Field hearing?' inquired Tolstoy. Tolstoy had learned that the original one had been postponed because Jack Bentley had had to have an emergency heart operation a week before the hearing, much to everyone's frustration.

'Do you know, I'm not sure. I've been so preoccupied with the funeral and everything that I had put it completely out of my mind. I shall ring the colonel shortly and find out.'

'Oh no, don't worry. I can always get in touch with him. I just wondered if a date had been set very recently, and that the colonel had not had time to contact me about it. After all, I am not exactly a regular attendee of committee meetings. So, no, please do not worry about it, you have enough on your plate already. Speaking of which, is there anything I can do?'

'Nothing that springs to mind immediately, and I am sure after the reading of the will tomorrow you will find yourself up to your neck in administration over the change of ownership of this place.'

Tolstoy found this a sobering thought. For the first time in his life he was about to become a home-owner. And not just of any home either, but Stottenden Manor, ending the ownership of generations of de Groots. He stared blankly out of the large window that overlooked the perfectly maintained garden at the rear of the Manor and gently shook his head in disbelief, bordering on bewilderment. To think all this was going to be his. He knew he would not be able to call it his until after the grant of probate, but even so, he was already beginning to feel the weight of responsibility. No matter how long it took to get probate, Tolstoy knew his duties to the house and to Elspeth began here and now. It was daunting.

Thus it was with a mixture of trepidation and excitement that he stepped into the solicitor's office the following day, a large room in a building creaking with age. The solicitor himself was the senior partner of the oldest established firm in the town, a spry man, with grey hair, who revealed a gentle, courteous manner as he guided Elspeth to a leather-covered chair while offering a welcoming smile for the two of them.

'Good morning Elspeth, Mr Pearce. It's good of you to come at such a harrowing time, but that is the way with things. Unfortunate, but there it is. They won't go away. Time and the law wait upon no man, one might say.'

He moved around the desk to sit opposite them, drew a file towards him and opened it. A brief shuffling of the documents contained therein produced the last will and testament of Hubert Jacobus Willem de Groot.

'As I am sure you are aware, Elspeth, Hubert used his final weeks wisely, sorting out all his finances in readiness for the taxman and I foresee very few last-minute hitches and glitches. Probate will still take time, probably a couple of months or so, but it should all be plain sailing.'

Financial provision had been made for Elspeth during the transitional period between death and probate, including funeral costs, and the solicitor insisted that should there be any emergency then Elspeth need merely to pick up a phone and let him know and funds would be made available.

'Now, Mr Pearce, I understand from Hubert that he made you aware of the fact that he was bequeathing you Stottenden Manor and its land, is that correct?'

Tolstoy found his throat appeared to be dry and he began by nodding, before adding somewhat croakily, 'Yes.'

'Would you like a glass of water?' asked the solicitor solicitously, and, before Tolstoy could reply, he was on his intercom and requesting a jug of water and glasses from his secretary.

While waiting for the drinks to appear he continued, 'Did Hubert tell you anything further about your inheritance?'

'Well not exactly. I mean, he explained that he wanted me to continue to maintain the cricket ground and uphold the traditions, supervise the various matches and so forth. And please call me Warren.'

'Thank you... Warren. No, no. I meant did he make you aware of the detail of his bequest to you?'

'No.' Tolstoy glanced at Elspeth in puzzlement; she merely smiled at him. 'No, not really.'

'Well, for example, did he make it clear that in leaving you Stottenden Manor he was also bequeathing to you all the fixtures and fittings, you know, the furniture, etc, not forgetting his wine cellar?'

'Um... I hadn't really thought about it, about that side of things.'

'And how about money? Did Hubert let you know he would be leaving you a not insubstantial sum of money?'

'No. No. He didn't. He didn't mention anything like that to me.'

'So how were you proposing to pay for the upkeep of Stottenden Manor, repairing it, painting it, keeping it watertight, and maintaining its grounds?' asked the solicitor gently.

'To be honest, that thought never crossed my mind. I mean, I suppose it might have eventually, when a problem arose, but it is actually quite difficult just coming to terms with the fact that Hubert has left me Stottenden. And the fact that I'm responsible for the cricket ground. It's going to be quite an undertaking. My only thought has been about how much time it might take sorting things out, making sure the pitches are properly prepared, that the outfield is mown regularly and the sight screens are painted before the start of each season, that the mowers and roller are serviced regularly, all that sort of thing. I don't suppose I could really think further than that.'

'Hmm... well...' at which point the office door opened and the secretary appeared, bearing a tray with a jug of water and three glasses. After placing them on the desk she withdrew and the solicitor did the honours. Tolstoy took a couple of gulps, wishing, in passing, that the glass contained a half-pint of Fuggles.

The solicitor took a sip from his glass before placing it back on the tray and continuing, 'Hubert enjoyed a great deal of success with his various investments. He was a canny, but prudent man. Risks were minimal, but he knew a good deal when he smelled one, and he had a great instinct for what was a good deal and what was not. Despite the several so-called financial crashes in his lifetime, his investments rarely suffered deep or long-term damage. As a result, he has been able to set up a number of trust funds, all of them substantial, providing a very generous income for Elspeth, and a handsome income for you, Warren. There is, additionally, a trust fund set up to fund the maintenance of the cricket ground and its pavilion, with provision for capital withdrawals to repair and/or replace the roller, mowers and other essential equipment as and when it should become necessary.

'These trust funds are in addition to a share portfolio, which is to be put in your name, Warren. I think it is safe to say that you will want for nothing.' At that point he furnished Tolstoy with a sheaf of accounts, which gave details of his riches. Tolstoy's eyes opened wide. Meanwhile the solicitor addressed the widow.

'Elspeth, I think you had already discussed the will with Hubert?'

'Yes. He had wanted to leave me more, but I have plenty already, far more than I need. And I know that Tolstoy, sorry Warren, has also agreed to allow me to remain in Stottenden, although he will become responsible financially, for all repairs and other charges relating to it, as well as taking over the day-to-day running of the place once we have the grant of probate, but for the time being I know I have to deal with all that sort of thing. Once Tolstoy does take over that will be a great relief to me. And, yes, I'm perfectly happy with what Hubert decided. I think it is only right and proper. We have no children. No nieces or nephews. Tolstoy is the nearest thing we have to a child of our own, and we both knew he would be the ideal person to inherit Stottenden and the cricket pitch. I think it is a perfect will. And more importantly, it was what Hubert dearly wanted, to leave all this to someone young enough, and with similar interests, to appreciate it and look after it for future generations. All that remains now, I suppose, is for Tolstoy to find a lovely young woman with whom to settle down in Stottenden and in time perhaps to produce children of his own to whom he can leave everything.'

They went into more detail with the solicitor, Elspeth produced more documents pertinent to probate and inheritance tax, then finally they were taking their leave, Tolstoy somewhat stunned at what he had inherited from his godfather, Elspeth relieved that she was coming to the end of the administrative duties that went hand in hand with the death of a loved one.

Once outside on the pavement she turned to Tolstoy and said, 'I think this calls for a celebration. We must raise a glass to Hubert for all that he has done for us.'

'Yes,' said Tolstoy, still feeling somewhat sandbagged by it all. He looked at his watch. 'It's lunchtime. What say we try that little pub Hubert said that you and he discovered in the spring?'

'Excellent idea. I think I can remember the way from here. Let's go.' They made their way around the back of the building to the solicitors' clients' car park and got into Elspeth's car and set off.

The pub was buzzing. It was very different from the Snitcher's Head. While an old building, possibly even older than the Snitcher's Head, it had had a recent makeover. A large conservatory had been added, as had an enormous wood-fired oven, in which the chef and his team were able to produce their own breads, pizzas and stone-cooked meats. There was a heavenly smell of garlic in the air, mingling with perfumes and wood smoke. It was, thought Tolstoy, a heady mix.

The pair of them settled at a table, Tolstoy with a pint, Elspeth with a sparkling water. They had made their choices for lunch – he a pizza, she a salad and fresh bread – and they clinked glasses.

'Well Tolstoy, it's happened. I had dreaded it, but in truth, after seeing the suffering that Hubert had to endure, I am frankly relieved that it's all over for him, and for me. All the admin has left me with precious little time to grieve, although, to tell you the truth, I have been doing my grieving since the original diagnosis. But I am just happy to be able to put it all behind me now. And we –you and I – now have things to discuss and plan.'

Tolstoy looked at her, eyebrows raised.

'Yes, I know. After last night there are yet more things to consider and make decisions about. I do seem to be laying down the law a bit, I'm sorry, but these things have to be talked about now. I think it's really important, for you, for me and not least for Stottenden Manor. And I can tell you that they are things that Hubert wanted me to discuss with you.' She stopped talking for a moment, removed a handkerchief from her handbag and dabbed delicately at her eyes. 'Sorry. It just hits me at unexpected times. I didn't want to embarrass you.' Her voice quavered.

Tolstoy patted her forearm gently. 'There's no need to apologise. I understand. And I know exactly what you mean about it coming up on you unexpectedly. Take your time.'

Elspeth smiled wanly. 'Thank you, Tolstoy. I think I'll be all right now, but I appreciate your understanding of my feelings. Hubert's death has really left a large hole in my life, and I don't know how I am going to fill it. I might need one or other of your shoulders from time to time, if that's all right?' Tolstoy nodded, and Elspeth picked up from where she had left off.

'As I was saying, Hubert felt that he wasn't up to talking about this himself, but he did make it very clear to me that I was to sit you down at the earliest opportunity and talk things through.'

'It all sounds a mite serious,' said Tolstoy warily.

'Well, that's because it is. I don't want to sound harsh, or unsympathetic, that's not my way, as you know. But you are now on the threshold of taking on some serious responsibilities, and in order to fulfil them you have to take certain actions in your own life, because, money apart, the biggest drain on you with the ownership of Stottenden Manor is time. You'll be surprised just how much of it the Manor will demand of you. This means you have to make possibly the most important decision of your life to date – you have to decide whether you need to give up your job in London and move down here permanently.'

Tolstoy sat upright, startled. 'Uh, that seems a bit drastic, Elspeth. I mean, I haven't even officially become the owner of the Manor yet.'

'No, but it is something to which I think you should give some thought. And it wasn't my idea, although I thought it was a good one; no, this is what Hubert thought made sense. Of course you don't have to stop work now, this minute, but you do need to consider it once we get the grant of probate. I can assure you that Hubert spent a couple of hours each morning on business related to the Manor and, lately, these trust funds. I'm afraid that you'll have to do the same. And if you carry on working in London you'll find that you'll be coming down to Stottenden most weekends and spending much of that time doing that sort of administration. I'm sorry if I'm sounding like a hard, unfeeling person. I'm just trying to help you to see what all this means. The fact is that what Hubert has left you means you won't need a job anymore.

'And anyway, what are your prospects in your job? Can you get promoted to a position of some responsibility? Could you end up as chairman? And, a further point, I think I am right in saying that you do not drive, yes?' There was a nod from Tolstoy. 'So you must organise driving lessons as soon as possible. But the most important thing you have to do is to make up your mind about your job. Is it really worth hanging onto it, when Stottenden awaits you, with, I can promise you, a busy enough schedule. After all, money will no longer be a deciding factor, now will it? So think hard about it, and then,' she smiled, 'hand in your notice.'

Tolstoy was about to launch into a defence of his job, when he paused, contemplated things a little more before engaging mouth, then finally addressed the issue. 'I suppose my prospects are not that great, really. The owner is unlikely to sell to me, and ordinarily even if he had offered me such an opportunity I would not have had the wherewithal to take him up on the offer. I have the title of "manager" but that is not a job description, that is a token title. There is just me, Darren, the company's archivist, and Kayleigh, a part-time secretary-cum-office manager, who sorts out the administrative side of things.

'It's interesting, but it can also be dull, and I suppose you could argue that I'm going nowhere. The money is poor. I've just never felt the need to move onwards and upwards. And these days no one wants to employ someone like me with a poor degree in business management.'

Elspeth spoke firmly, but kindly. 'Well, once you take over down here I can promise you there will be plenty to occupy you. I think you'll find that Hubert actually wrote out a list, well actually, dictated a list, to me, of tasks you'll need to do almost daily. You will not receive that lot until the grant of probate, but when you do I think you'll be surprised, if not a little shocked. How much notice do you have to give?'

'Only a month, I think. I'm not really sure. But I'm also not sure that I'm ready for this.'

'Have a chat with friends. Charlie Hornchurch for one. He has his head screwed on and he understands what you are taking on down here.'

'But Charlie works in the City, and he has a serious pile to look after as well. Why do I need to stop work?' Even to Tolstoy's ears that last question sounded more like a childish whine than a reasoned argument.

Being the lady that she was, Elspeth took the question at face value. 'Charlie has a team of people working on the estate. He probably only needs to devote a few hours each month, perhaps signing a few documents and so on. Down here there will be only you, because I have never run the house and grounds, and I can assure you that, while I am prepared to do some basic day-to-day running for the time being, the moment we get probate you will be taking over. After all Hubert did everything, and I know he expected you to do the same when you took over.'

At that point their food arrived, which gave a chastened Tolstoy more time to think things over. Initially he was humbled into silence. He had to admit he knew he had been going nowhere for some time, but lethargy, apathy, call it what you will, seemed to rule his life these days. He took a mouthful of pizza. The fact that there was no "significant other" gently goading him into being a trifle more ambitious probably did not help, he reasoned to himself. But his hours were also a handicap. He started work late morning, or, more often, around midday, then worked until maybe 9pm. There was the occasional Saturday or Sunday call-out, of which there had been rather more than usual over the last couple of months, he reflected. His time never really seemed to be his own; it was as if he were just sitting in his flat, or in the office, waiting for a request to be phoned in.

Another bite of pizza and another thoughtful chew. He invariably picked up a sandwich or a takeaway meal on his way home and once that had been consumed he went to bed. He saw no one, other than his landlady when he paid the rent once a quarter. It was a soulless existence. Yes, that's what it was, an existence, not a life. He had thought about learning to cook to try to improve his diet, but somehow he just could not be bothered even to look into days and times of cookery courses. Maybe now was the time to do something about it all. And once he got into the swing of things at Stottenden there might even be a part-time job that he could undertake locally. He had to admit that he was not exactly happy in his job. It was a fairly thankless occupation. More pizza. And living in Stottenden, as his own boss, so to speak, would mean that there would probably be more opportunity to watch cricket at Canterbury, Hove, Tunbridge Wells, Horsham, even The Oval and Lord's, for that matter, or perhaps further afield, without having to use up holiday allocation to do so. After all, in order to come down and give some moral support to Elspeth he had had to take unpaid leave. Unpaid leave in the twenty-first century, for something like this? It was not as if he was taking time off to go to Las Vegas and blow his pittance of a salary on The Strip. He was taking the time off for someone else. To be there for them. But his boss had insisted there could be no compassionate, paid, leave. Now though, things did seem a little brighter. A couple more mouthfuls of pizza fuelled further thoughts. No. Things looked a lot brighter. Spring and summer would hold far more for him from now on. All he had to do was embrace his new role. Accept his new status, socially and financially. And Elspeth had merely been conveying Hubert's thoughts on the matter. She was sympathetic, he could see and hear it. She had also been diplomatic in the way she had phrased things. There was no admonishment in her voice. She was just her usual gentle self. And there was really no one else close enough to Tolstoy who could, and would, say what needed to be said.

Tolstoy pushed himself away from the table and sat back in his chair. 'Thank you, Elspeth. I think you are right. I have been putting off this debate with myself about my situation for far too long. It's a very easy thing to do when you are on your own. Well, when you live on your own. I'm in a job that's going nowhere. How long did the solicitor say probate would take?'

'I think about three months.'

'Right then, I shall give my boss two months' notice when I'm back at work and I shall sort out moving out of my flat and shifting my belongings down here. Will that be OK?'

'That will be perfect, Tolstoy. That should give you some time to get your feet under the table, so to speak.'

Elspeth meanwhile had finished her salad and watched as Tolstoy polished off the remains of his pizza. They ordered a coffee and chatted about their surroundings and the way pubs had changed in the last couple of decades. Finally Elspeth said they should head back to Stottenden, when she would ring the colonel for the latest news on the Buttercup Field hearing.

The colonel was unable to enlighten Elspeth. 'All I can tell you is that it will be this year,' he explained. 'The inspectorate is having to find a slot for us in what they tell me is an extremely busy schedule. It is a bit of a nuisance because we all have to make plans and re-organise our own work schedules to fit it in, and there is now a possibility that we may have to find another barrister, because there is no guarantee that Angela Smeaton will be available, since she could well be involved in a case. And I cannot see any judge suspending a court case and releasing a barrister to come down to Kent for a hearing such as ours. It's all rather worrying. I've been assured that a decision will be made very soon and that I'll be informed the moment anything is decided. I promise I shall let everyone know the moment I hear.'

Tolstoy grimaced at the news. 'Just what no one wants, for this thing to drag on. By the way, how is Jack Bentley? What with Hubert and everything else I had forgotten all about him. Has he made a full recovery?'

Elspeth cocked her head to one side. 'Do you know, I haven't given him another thought either, for pretty much the same reason as you. I've been so wrapped up in Hubert's final few weeks and then the funeral arrangements and all the administrative chores, that Jack's health has not crossed my mind. As far as I recall he had a triple or quadruple bypass and was expected to have to take things easy for a few weeks. I'm sure I would have heard if he had had a relapse, so I think it is safe to assume he is continuing to recover, and no doubt we shall see him swanning around in one or other of his ostentatious cars, pronouncing on this, that or any other thing which he feels demands his opinion. Oh I can't bear the man. Such a snob. And a bit of a bully too. He has certainly behaved poorly over the Buttercup Field.'

Tolstoy raised an eyebrow as Elspeth's tirade ended, leaving her pink-cheeked and looking indignant.

'I'm sorry, Tolstoy. I don't know where all that came from. But the man really does get under my skin.

'So, as a complete change of subject, let us move to matters more mundane. When you move in here would you prefer the master bedroom? I am perfectly happy to move to one of the guest rooms.'

'Oh good heavens, no,' Tolstoy protested. 'That's your room. I have no intention of turfing you out of the bedroom you have used for the last however many years it is. I shall be quite content to use my usual room. It has an *en suite* and I am familiar with it.'

'Thank you, Tolstoy, that is really sweet and thoughtful of you. I don't mind moving, but I have all my clothes and things there. So thank you. I do wonder, though, whether it might be nice to redecorate both bedrooms, yours and mine. It's been years since they last had a lick of paint. Would you mind if I organised that to be completed in time for when you move in?'

'No, that would be fine.'

'I suppose we ought to be going through all Hubert's papers and things, especially all the documents and accounts relating to the Manor,' said Elspeth. 'Or would you rather leave all that for the time being?'

'I think leave it for the time being. I think I may head back to London sooner than planned to sort out handing in my notice to my boss and to my landlady,' said Tolstoy. 'I rather think I will be able to get away within a month, but I need to organise moving my belongings from the flat down here as well. Would it be OK to come down perhaps the weekend after next?'

'Warren, Stottenden Manor is *your* home now, so you can come and go as you please.'

'I know, but I think I still owe you the courtesy of letting you know when I intend popping down. At least until I move in permanently.'

'Thank you, I appreciate that. And the weekend after next will be fine. Oh,' she paused, lips pursed, then went on, 'I knew there was something I wanted to tell you. Charlie Hornchurch has been a regular down here since the cricket match. Initially he stayed either at the Star and Eagle, or in the Snitcher's Head, but last weekend he was actually a guest of the Charleses.'

Tolstoy looked surprised. 'Really?'

'Yes, it seems he has been seeing Henrietta when up in London. They have also been coming down to her family home, which is between here and Goudhurst, and going for walks and so on. More recently she has been coming down every weekend to stay with her parents while her flat is being refurbished. During the week she stays in a small hotel in the West End when she is working. According to Vivienne, her mother, she and Charlie are really rather keen on each other.'

Tolstoy had mixed emotions. He was glad that Charlie had finally, possibly, met someone, but also sad that a woman he found so breathtakingly beautiful – not that he had spared her a thought since the day he had introduced himself by standing on her hair – should be seeing another man, and that that man was his closest friend. In fact, it was odd that Charlie had not mentioned it at the funeral. Why was that? Tolstoy could answer that one himself. On the day of the funeral he had slipped away as quickly as he could, and had barely said two words to Charlie on that emotionally-charged day. Well, maybe they would bump into each other a little more now, if Charlie Hornchurch and Henrietta Charles were now an "item", always assuming the couple spent time together at her parents' home, because very shortly now Tolstoy would be coming down to spend the rest of his life at Stottenden. He marvelled at the thought. He had to admit that he did rather relish the prospect. And was even, if he were to be honest, rather excited at the thought.

SIX

Tolstoy stepped into the welcoming, relative darkness of the Snitcher's Head and made his way across the near-empty room to the bar. As ever Jo was there, bending down to stock up some lower shelves. She had heard the door open and close though, and she quickly straightened up and turned to look at Tolstoy. 'Tolstoy, how are you? When do you move in permanently? And what on earth have you been doing, your face is black, well almost. Have you had an early bonfire? Bonfire Night isn't for a couple of weeks, you know.'

Tolstoy pulled out a bright red handkerchief and wiped his face. 'Sorry. No. There has been no bonfire, I've been in the cellar all morning, the larger bit of the cellar that doesn't have any wine in it, shifting and dragging stuff around and raising a regular old dust storm.

'I promised Elspeth I would brave the spiders and the dust to see what lay in the darkest depths of Stottenden Manor, and I have uncovered a little treasure trove of three trunks, two suitcases and half a dozen wine boxes. The trunks look old, in fact one of them looks positively antique, and were hidden behind a wooden screen tucked away into one of the furthest, darkest corners of the cellar. I had to go back upstairs for a torch in order to see just what I had found. They could not have been looked at in years, if not decades. In fact, I suspect in a couple of instances, some of the boxes, and the very large, old-fashioned trunk, might have not been opened for centuries. Anyway, as a result of all that labouring I am exhausted. Thirsty. Grubby. So I have given myself a brief beer break before joining Elspeth for lunch. And in answer to your first two questions, fine, and I have just moved in permanently this week, so I am still finding my feet. But I am getting there, and Elspeth is a great companion and, more importantly, a superb cook.'

Throughout his explanation Jo had been pulling him a pint of Fuggles. Tolstoy looked at her; she seemed different. She had smiled at him, but something was different in the smile. She took his money, opened the till and dropped in the coins, then, instead of engaging Tolstoy in conversation she moved to the other end of the bar, where Tolstoy noticed a figure seated on a bar stool reading a magazine. When the figure looked up Tolstoy saw that it was Harry Stoke, and a smile creased his face as Jo murmured something to him. He turned and looked at Tolstoy and nodded at him.

'Afternoon, Mr Pearce.' The voice was low and cut through with a pleasant West Country burr.

'Good afternoon, Harry, and please, it's Warren, or even Tolstoy if you're of a mind to use my nickname.'

'Thank you... Tolstoy.'

'How's the shooting season going?'

'Good. Very good. Hard work of course. I'm just stealing half an hour to see Jo, before I head off to check one of the drives we plan on using tomorrow. Do you shoot, Tolstoy?'

'No, I'm afraid not. It's not that I'm anti or anything. It's just not something that has ever really grabbed me. I enjoy eating game though, especially venison and partridge.'

'Well, we've opened a shoot shop and you can get pretty well all game there. You should pay us a visit. Jo here runs it, so it's only open three mornings a week, but the meat is all oven-ready.'

Harry turned back to Jo, draining his glass as he did so, then said, 'Well sweetheart, I'm off. See you this evening.'

He leaned across the bar and managed a kiss that clearly pleased Jo, before hauling his towering frame off the stool and heading to the door. Jo came back up to Tolstoy's end and eyed his glass. It was half-empty. 'You want a top-up?'

Tolstoy hesitated. 'I really shouldn't. Oh, what the hell! Yes. But just a top-up.'

He began fishing in his pocket for some change, but Jo stopped him, saying, 'Have this one on me,' and filled his glass. And while she did so she began talking about Harry. 'He hates Bonfire Night.'

'Who does?'

'Harry. He says it's an invitation for poachers to come out and blast away at game birds and deer and no one can tell what's going on, or where. He'll be out there next week, patrolling the shoot, the parts of it that he thinks are vulnerable to poachers; the places where the pheasants roost are favourite for poachers to go. Often, Harry says, this sort of poaching is just locals out to get something free for the larder. I hated selling fireworks in the shop. Too often

I was suspicious of the age of some of the youngsters and I was scared of selling them to underage children.' She tailed off as she finished filling the glass.

'Forgive me for being nosey, Jo, but how many jobs do you have now? I know you do a paper round, serve in the village shop and then do lunchtimes and evenings here, but now you are running the shoot's shop as well. How on earth do you fit it all in?'

'I don't think you're nosey, Warren. In fact, if I hadn't been swept off my feet by Harry a while back you might have found yourself stepping out with me and learning all about my life, because I think you are one of the sweetest men I have met, well, along with Harry, of course. I've given up working in the shop altogether, which includes stopping the paper round; those jobs served a purpose, they helped me to put together a nice little nest egg, but I love my job here, meeting everyone, hearing all the gossip. Being around people. I just have a slightly later start three mornings a week to allow me to run the shoot's shop. I open that at eight, close it at midday. Then by twelve-fifteen I am in here.'

Tolstoy, still taken aback at having been called sweet, just managed to stutter, 'So... so... so do you still have ambitions to leave the village, like you always said you would?'

'I'm not so sure. Now that Harry and I are seeing each other. We have even been talking, but just talking, about moving in together. In my cottage. I own it now, so there's no mortgage or anything to worry about. And although the colonel is very kind to Harry, the cottage that he lives in for free is not his. He says he wants a little more of a permanent feeling, a permanent place to stay. We think maybe if we make a go of things between us, that we might end up... you know... getting married or something.' She paused. It had been a long speech for her and Jo appeared quite exhausted, not to say a trifle self-conscious, at her personal revelations. But there was more to come.

'I think that is truly lovely that you and Harry are together,' said Tolstoy, and meaning it. 'He seems a nice chap. Although I'll bet he works really long hours.'

'He is. He's out at all hours. He gets up sometimes at two, three or four in the morning and I always wake up.' She stopped suddenly, aware that she had revealed something rather more personal than perhaps she had intended and she blushed deeply. Ever the gentleman, Tolstoy chose not to react to this personal revelation. He actually felt himself blush as well, as if he had been caught eavesdropping. Despite his initial attraction to Jo, it was Kate, of whom he had seen very little over the past four months or so, who now interested him more. Not that the feelings had been reciprocated thus far. 'Is the game that you sell in the shoot's shop good quality?'

'Oh yes. And we usually have pretty well everything, pheasant, duck, partridge, pigeon, rabbit, and of course venison, oh and wild goose when in season. You or Elspeth should drop in.'

Tolstoy emptied his glass and promised Jo he would call in the next time it was open. 'That'll be tomorrow. Any time after eight,' she said.

'See you then. Bye.' And with that he left.

During lunch, at the start of which he had suggested that Elspeth might like to sample some game from the shoot's shop, they discussed what he had discovered in the cellar so far, and just what the cases, trunks and boxes might contain. 'I don't think even Hubert could remember what was in them,' she said. 'Although I do recall that one of them contains accounts for the Manor going back donkey's years. Hubert kept saying he ought to read through them, if nothing else just to see how costs of maintenance have risen. He did say it would probably depress him, but, other than that, I have no idea what you may find.'

'Would you care to join me in the cellar to have a first-hand browse?'

'I might pop down later, but I have one or two things I must get done this afternoon, including a little bit of shopping for this evening's meal. And I have rather neglected my reading. I belong to a book club and I must get on with our latest book. Unusually for the club, rather than it being a serious, or high-minded work of non-fiction – we do read a lot of historical biographies – this one is a thriller, by a local author, C J Bateman. It's his latest one. He lives somewhere in the South East, and that is generally the setting for his stories. His first one, for example, was set on the Kent and Sussex coast. It was very good too. Anyway, with all this, you go ahead with your dusty duties. I doubt if I will find the time to join you later. But while I think about it, would you like to borrow some gloves? I have Hubert's old gardening gloves or a pair of rubber gloves out in the scullery.'

'No, I'll be fine with bare hands, even if they will get fairly grubby. Do you need a hand with the washing-up?'

'No. Most of it can go in the dishwasher. You get on with your dusty duties.'

Tolstoy grinned, got up from the kitchen table and went over to the heavy cellar door, switched on the lights, opened the door and made his way down the flagstone steps. As he made his way between the racks and bins of wine he made a mental note to take a bottle or two back with him later to accompany the evening meal.

Earlier he had taken a chair down with him to spare himself the discomfort of squatting, and now he dragged two of the cardboard boxes over and began examining the contents. The first one was only half-full, and contained, as far as he could see, a collection of A5 cards, which featured addresses, in alphabetical order. Tolstoy pushed it to one side for Elspeth to check over. The second one, again nowhere near full, had some old computer magazines. *Rubbish*, thought Tolstoy, pushing this box to the right. Two more boxes were hauled through the dust, both crammed with Wine Society quarterly catalogues. As tempting as it would have been to hang on to these, just to see how much prices of various wines had changed, Tolstoy decided to be ruthless and consigned both to the right-hand side of his chair.

The last two seemed to hold desktop knickknacks, paperweights, blotters, a desk lamp and three computer keyboards, as well as a clutch of ballpoint pens and some pencils. Again Tolstoy pushed them to his right.

The trunks were what had filled him with curiosity, and so it was with a frisson of anticipation that he dragged the first one across the cellar floor, raising yet more dust clouds. The lid was fastened by a simple hasp, there was no locking mechanism and Tolstoy was able to open it with no trouble. Although it had felt fairly heavy, to Tolstoy's disappointment all that it contained was what appeared to be bundles of old curtains, made of heavy, silk brocade material.

With a sigh he pushed the trunk to his left, for Elspeth to decide on the fate of its contents at some point. The second trunk was clearly empty, judging by the way it felt. Impatiently Tolstoy pushed that to one side to clear the way for the third. This one certainly felt as if it contained something. Again, there was no lock, so Tolstoy quickly found himself staring at some papers. Old documents. Trembling, Tolstoy pulled out a handful and began to leaf through them. After about ten minutes, when he was getting on for halfway through, it dawned on him that these were all old annual accounts for Stottenden Manor. The further he went through the more obvious it also became that they had been filed in chronological order, and he was now in the late 1890s. He decided to make an executive decision and delved almost to the very bottom of the pile. Here he reached the year 1842. Queen Victoria had been on the throne for five years, and Stottenden Manor's finances were looking as sound as they were almost two hundred years later. It seemed that Hubert's great-great-grandfather and great-grandfather were canny managers of the modest estate and prudent with the spending. At the very bottom of the pile he came upon accounts relating to the mid-eighteenth century, Hubert's great-great-great-great-grandfather's time. Tolstoy felt a thrill. He was holding history in his hands, he marvelled. Leafing forward again, Tolstoy uncovered the accounts for the year the original pavilion had been built. The construction had cost a shade under £75 in total, in 1863, with the help of lots of volunteer labour.

The accounts were of interest, Tolstoy decided, so he eased the trunk to his left. Lastly he had the two suitcases to look at. They were another disappointment, all they contained were old clothes – no surprise there, thought Tolstoy, given their usual role in life. Tolstoy sat back in the chair. He glanced at his watch and saw that almost two hours had elapsed. He felt thirsty and his eyes felt gritty. His face was also covered in sweat and he wiped a handkerchief across his forehead and upper lip. He would have to ask Elspeth where she wanted him to put the boxes and trunks that he thought she needed to look through.

He stood up and turned towards the stairs. Access to them involved having to move the empty trunk. Except Tolstoy had not actually checked it to see if it really was empty. Perhaps he should, so with an involuntary groan he squatted by the trunk and lifted the lid. It wasn't empty.

There was not much in it, but there was enough to excite Tolstoy, because what he could see was a large, brown legal type of envelope. There was nothing else, though. He reached in and pulled it out. It was addressed to Cornelis de Groot of Stottenden Manor in faded ink. Hubert's grandfather, or his great-great-great grandfather he thought, since they both had the same Christian name. There was no stamp on the front, nor postmark. He turned the envelope over, but there was nothing to say where it had come from. He decided that this was something worth taking upstairs and studying over a cup of tea with Elspeth. She might even recognise it. A sharp shove cleared the way for Tolstoy to exit the cellar up the stairs back to the kitchen.

When he got there, there was no sign of Elspeth, but a quick call from him established that she was in the library and she said she would join him and provide him with a cup of tea.

'Any joy?' she asked, when she came through the kitchen door.

'I'm not sure, but I think this might be interesting.' Tolstoy handed her the dusty envelope. 'Good gracious,' exclaimed Elspeth. 'It's addressed to Hubert's grandfather. Well, or his great-great-great-grandfather of course, since they were both called Cornelis de Groot.' As Tolstoy had done, she turned the envelope over, before slipping her fingers in the open end and withdrawing some extremely old-looking documents.

'Well, I wonder what these are,' she mused. Still holding them she went over to the sink and brought back a cloth, with which she wiped the surface of the kitchen table before carefully placing the first batch on it. She withdrew the remaining documents and laid these out on the pine surface as well.

'Do you mind if I look at one?' she asked Tolstoy.

'No, go ahead. I brought them up here really so that you could have a first look at them, in case you knew what they were.'

Elspeth pulled up a chair, Tolstoy likewise, and she reached out for what looked to be the oldest, or at least most yellowed, document in the collection. It was not very large, but appeared to be a letter. It was.

'It's from the family's firm of solicitors in Tonbridge,' she announced. 'It's dated 1911. November 14th.' She began to read. '*Dear Cornelis, Please find enclosed the documents you requested. You may keep them, unless you would prefer to return them to our sturdy office safe. The two relevant plans you felt sure were included among the deeds to Stottenden Manor, were indeed there and they are self-explanatory, one is dated before, the other after, the changes were made. Your grandfather, Willem, clearly created a smaller field as some sort of shield from the road, to help enclose the cricket ground...* It then goes on about local cricket and various social bits and bobs. So where are these two plans?'

While Elspeth had been reading out from the solicitor's letter Tolstoy had been carefully unfolding a couple of the dry pieces of paper. The third one that he opened looked like a plan. A black ink outline of an area with two lines running parallel and close together at the bottom, and a smallish square shape on the top left-hand side. There was writing, but it was extremely small. Tolstoy had to squint hard. 'Oh! Oh! I think this is the cricket field and this square thing at the top is Stottenden Manor. It's obviously not to scale.'

Elspeth asked, 'But what is all that writing down the side, in the right-hand margin? It's really small. Whoever produced this plan must have had fantastic eyesight, I can't read a word.'

Tolstoy grunted, 'Nor can I. Do you have a magnifying glass?'

'I think there's one on the desk in the library. If it's not on the desk, then the chances are that it will be in the top left-hand drawer.'

Tolstoy headed down the corridor to the oak-panelled library. The desk sat in front of the large window, opposite the doorway. He made his way over to the other side of the desk and spotted the magnifying glass on the left of the blotter. He picked it up and returned to the kitchen, to find that Elspeth had found and unfolded the second of the plans mentioned in the solicitor's letter. He passed her the magnifying glass and waited while she peered through it at the first plan.

'That's better,' she said. 'It says, *Being a plan of the land adjoining and owned by Willem de Groot of Stottenden Manor, Stottenden, in the County of Kent.* Well now, Willem de Groot was Hubert's great-great-grandfather, so it looks as if he owned all the land that ran right up to the road.'

'Is that what it's saying?' queried Tolstoy. 'Because if it is, then all this hoo-hah over the Buttercup Field may be over, and the parish council plans to annex it as their own and do all that building on it will come to nought.'

Elspeth looked flushed. 'This is very exciting. Let's see what the other plan shows.'

'Is there any writing on the second one?'

'Yes, there is. But this plan is rather different. Look, here someone has drawn a line parallel to what is obviously the road that runs through the village. It looks as if it has created a smaller field, by taking a chunk out of the cricket field. And those little dash-type things, on the top and bottom of the new field, could very well be the gates that are there today. That's the one that is on the roadside,' she explained, pointing with the tip of her long, elegant forefinger, 'and that's the other, right opposite, the one that leads directly into the cricket field. Let's see what this writing says. *Being a plan of the proposed gift in perpetuo to the parish of St Martin's Church Stottenden and its parishioners of a parcel of land no fewer than two and one half acres and no more than three acres, from Willem de Groot for the common weal. Dated this day September 17th in the year of our Lord 1839.* It has been witnessed, presumably by someone from Stottenden and someone from the church, perhaps the vicar. It has also been dated, and to my eye it all looks official.' Elspeth's hand trembled with excitement as she picked up the plan and studied it more closely. 'Well Tolstoy, this is good news, because it means the de Groots gave what became known as the Buttercup Field to the Church, to St Martin's. So you are right. And that puts an end to the nonsense of the parish council, or anyone, doing anything, let alone building houses there. We simply must tell the colonel.' Tolstoy held up a cautionary hand. 'I think that Jack Bentley and his fellow councillors will call it mighty convenient that, with matters coming to a head, we should unearth these documents. I'll bet they accuse us of nefarious deeds, perhaps even of forging them.'

'Oh, Tolstoy, I didn't know you could be so cynical.'

'I'm not being cynical, just realistic. I think we would be well advised to keep this quiet for the time being, just while we find somewhere that we can have these plans and the letter authenticated. We should be able to get them dated at least. I am sure there are forensic establishments who do private work like this every week.'

'Hmm, well perhaps the remaining documents can help to verify that what we have here is genuine,' said Elspeth, and she began carefully to unfold another piece of paper. A five-minute perusal of the remaining documents proved useful in one way, in that they formed a chain of correspondence between Willem de Groot and his solicitor, leading ultimately to the change of plan and the registration of the new boundary. There was also a letter, rather a curt one, from the Diocese of Canterbury acknowledging the Church's gratitude for the land and thanking Willem de Groot for his generous gift.

'These should all prove useful,' said the optimistic Tolstoy, 'because no one could have forged them all, and they should, in the right forensic hands, reinforce the dates of the plans and the covering letter.'

Elspeth agreed. 'How do we go about finding a firm, or someone, to examine and date all these? And how much is it all going to cost? I'm certain of one thing, it's not going to be cheap.'

'I don't think the onus is on us to prove the authenticity of any of these documents,' said Tolstoy. 'Not legally anyway. Morally maybe. I think we'll just have to produce them for the parish council and let them have the documents authenticated, maybe let the cost come out of the communal purse, rather than ours. We'll have a think about it.'

Elspeth accorded Tolstoy some muted applause. 'That is brilliant, Tolstoy. Yes, why indeed should we have to prove anything? We have found the documents; it is for others to challenge their veracity. When should they be presented to the council, do you think?'

'Well, I should like us to invite the colonel and his wife around for a drink, show him the documents, get his opinion. Who knows, he might be able to suggest a reliable forensics outfit somewhere. We also need to let Reverend Davis know about all this. And we need to invite them all before we present these documents to the parish council. I also wonder whether we should get these photocopied and present the copies to the council and Jack Bentley Esq; after all we do not want these delicate pieces of paper, on which the future existence of the Buttercup Field rests, to be damaged by mishandling, or, worse, have someone "lose" them. It would also be good if we made another set of copies and showed them, again, before we present them to the PC, to the members of the action committee, who have all been so supportive throughout this campaign. And, despite what I have just said about the onus being on the council to authenticate the documents, on reflection I think it would be worth our while paying to have them authenticated ourselves, just for our own peace of mind.'

Elspeth had an even more ambitious idea. 'Perhaps you're right about the Manor footing the bill for the authentication, and I agree about showing them to the colonel first at drinks here, but how about inviting, not just the committee, but the whole village to a big party, maybe in a marquee on the cricket field?'

'That is a great idea, Elspeth,' said Tolstoy, 'but we don't want to tempt providence. The party is a great idea, but let's have that once these documents have been authenticated and Jack Bentley and the parish council have conceded defeat. After all, it would be terrible if it turned out that the documents weren't genuine, or were not acceptable legally for whatever arcane reason the council's solicitors could dream up.'

Elspeth agreed. 'OK, a compromise. First the colonel, then the Rev Davis, followed by the action committee, then a meeting in the Snitcher's Head of all the villagers, which I do realise will mean a couple of parish councillors attending, and letting them know that we think we have evidence that will save the Buttercup Field, but we don't say what the evidence is. How does that sound?'

'Perfect,' said a happy Tolstoy.

'I shall sort out a possible date for the colonel and Miriam to drop in for drinks, maybe tomorrow or perhaps they might be able to join us at the weekend, Sunday lunchtime perhaps?' She looked at Tolstoy questioningly. He nodded his approval.

'Right, Tolstoy,' said Elspeth in a firm tone. 'I want you to go down to the cellar again,' she paused, and Tolstoy, who had been looking forward to a shower to rid himself of the dirt that coated him after his efforts below ground, looked up with a despairing face, only to hear Elspeth add, 'and dig out something appropriate for a celebration. It may not yet be a *fait accompli*, but you and I know those documents are genuine, so we can jolly well quaff a glass or two ourselves. What do you say?'

'I am on my way down as you speak.'

'And get something to go with steak and béarnaise sauce, which we are having tonight.'

'Will do.'

It took Tolstoy some half a dozen minutes to decide on what fizz and what wines to drink, and when he emerged from the cellar, he was confronted by a grinning Elspeth. 'I'm afraid I have to ask you to pop down to the cellar again, Tolstoy, and fetch more of the same, perhaps a further two more of the same, because while you were down there I had a phone call. Charlie Hornchurch is popping over with Henrietta Charles. They are coming as much to see you as me. Initially they were just going to drop in for a quick drink, but I pressed them to stay for a meal. There is plenty of steak and salad and chips. I hope you don't mind. They said they'd be here at about seven.'

Tolstoy had groaned inwardly, and perhaps there had momentarily even been a flicker, just a flicker, of displeasure that had passed across his face at Elspeth's first words, but he managed to get himself under control in time to hear the rest of her news. And he smiled at the prospect of seeing his old friend again. It really had been too long since they last met, which had been at Hubert's funeral.

'No problem,' and he turned around and, for the umpteenth time that day, disappeared into the bowels of Stottenden Manor.

SEVEN

The ancient front door bell at Stottenden Manor clanged sonorously at three minutes to seven. Elspeth left Tolstoy to sort out the glasses and the wine and went to answer it. Tolstoy heard the voices, then thirty seconds later was greeting his old friend and shaking hands for only the second time in his life with Henrietta Charles as they entered the kitchen.

'I believe you two know each other,' said Charlie.

'Um, yes,' Tolstoy managed.

'You could say that,' came the dusky tones of Henrietta. 'Although our first meeting was not exactly a happy one.'

'Oh? Why was that?' asked Charlie and a bemused Elspeth, in unison. Elspeth, after all, had thought that Tolstoy and Henrietta had met through her at the cricket match.

Tolstoy blushed fiercely and spared himself from answering by asking if Henrietta would like some champagne. She nodded, before turning to Charlie and relating her first encounter with Tolstoy, or rather a clumsy, oversized part of his anatomy. Within seconds both Elspeth and Charlie were chuckling, so well did Henrietta recall the incident of Tolstoy standing on her hair. She didn't miss a beat, not even when she was handed her glass of bubbly. When she had finished Henrietta turned to Tolstoy and added, 'You're forgiven, by the way. And, for your information, it didn't hurt me at all. It merely annoyed me that anyone could fail to spot my hair, and it is pretty hard to miss after all, and then to stand on it to boot. Well, it was all rather too much for me, I'm afraid. Although I do think that I was possibly a little harsh on you. Never mind. And no harm done.'

A near-mute Tolstoy merely hung his head, before managing a mumbled 'Sorry.'

Charlie broke the brief silence by asking, 'Why the bubbly? Are we celebrating something?'

'In a way,' said Elspeth. 'We can't actually reveal what it is, because it needs confirmation, but Tolstoy here has unearthed something which could end this whole Buttercup Field affair, in favour of the village. If what he has uncovered is right, then Jack Bentley and his fellow parish councillors will not be able to build anything on the Buttercup Field. But right now it has to be kept secret from everyone, especially the local councillors. We need to be sure of our facts before we make the discovery public, and that is going to take a bit of time.'

'Right ho,' said Charlie, raising his glass. 'A toast to whatever it is that Tolstoy has found, and long may the Buttercup Field retain its status.' They all raised their glasses, then sipped to the toast. 'Actually, it's rather strange that you should have mentioned the name Jack Bentley,' said

Charlie, 'because we have just come from the Snitcher's Head, where we had a swift yardarm libation, and the talk there was of that selfsame man. Jack was in the bar, but at the far end talking to a couple of his farm workers, so thankfully we did not have to talk directly to him, but he was the topic of the day, all right.'

'Really,' said Elspeth. 'What was being said about him?'

'Well, apparently he seems to think he has found documentary proof that shows his great-great-grandfather, Edward Bentley, was given the Buttercup Field by a member of the de Groot family back in the mid-19th century. Old Jack is going to present it to the parish council at their next meeting in a fortnight's time, after which he will hand it over to the PC's legal people who can then sort out the granting of planning consent, and of course this will then render the public inquiry a non-starter.'

'Good gracious,' exclaimed Elspeth, her face an indignant pink. 'That's not possible. Just not possible.' She wanted to say more, but a warning glance from Tolstoy ensured she did not. Charlie, slightly startled at the vehemence of Elspeth's outburst, continued, 'I can assure you that Jack is behaving like the cat that got the cream. He could not stop smiling. He was surrounded by his cronies and some of his employees. He was slapping people on the back, buying them drinks. He was definitely in a celebratory mood. And you know how obnoxious his smile of triumph can be. He really was buzzing earlier.'

'Oh, good heavens, enough talk of that vile man,' said Elspeth. 'With what Tolstoy has found, I am certain it will prevail over anything that that vulgar man Jack Bentley is going to produce. Now, let's just please change the subject.'

She turned to Charlie's girlfriend. 'Henrietta, how is work with you?'

'It's fine. Good, in fact. I have just been offered a staff job, which is tempting. I'm presently on a contract, which is useful from a tax point of view, but the staff job carries more responsibility, more hours' work as well as a reasonably generous increase in pay. I have been given the weekend to consider it, but I am going to discuss it with my parents, and Charlie.'

'It sounds wonderful, Henrietta. But I think you're wise to want to hear what your parents and Charlie here have to say before you go jumping in and saying yes or no.' She turned to Charlie. 'And what news of you, Charlie? How's the new job going?'

'Far better than I had anticipated. I'm running a good team of financial analysts and we have enjoyed a fair amount of success over the last few months, which should be reflected in my bonus at the year end. The hours are fairly long, but that doesn't bother me, well, it hadn't bothered me until recently, when I began seeing more of young Henry.' He turned to Henrietta and smiled. To Tolstoy's eyes she seemed to melt under his friend's gaze, and he could not help but feel the faintest twinge of envy, partly because his best friend had found a partner, and was clearly extremely in love, and partly because of his own attraction to Henrietta. Meanwhile, he remained single. Since officially moving in to Stottenden Manor he had not set eyes on Kate, and what with Jo, whom he had briefly entertained the thought of asking out, now clearly settling down with Harry Stoke, Tolstoy was feeling rather neglected and alone. He gave a mental shrug.

'Is everyone happy staying in here?' asked Elspeth. There were nods of assent. 'Good, that means I won't miss out on any of the conversation.' She looked up at Charlie, then at Henrietta, specifically, Henrietta's left hand. 'Oh my goodness! Is that an engagement ring?'

'It looks more like a boulder,' quipped Tolstoy, in a rare moment of humour, as Henrietta held up her left hand for inspection. There on the ring finger of her left hand could be seen a diamond, the size of a large pebble, surrounded by, as far as Tolstoy could tell, more, but slightly smaller, pebble-sized diamonds, set in yellow gold. It was big. It was obviously expensive. And it was definitely a permanent-looking fixture, auguring well for the forthcoming union, thought Tolstoy, who, not for the first time recently, wondered just how wealthy his old friend actually was. Of course he would never ask Charlie how much the ring had cost, but the mind boggled around the five figure mark, or maybe more.

'Um, yes,' said Charlie, in response to Elspeth's question. 'That was actually the reason for dropping in on you like this. I popped the question a few days ago, was accepted by "H" and last night I gained the approval of her parents.'

'Well, congratulations both of you,' said Elspeth.

'Yes, jolly well done, you two,' said Tolstoy with a huge smile. 'Now we have even more reason to carry on with the bubbly. Have you set a date yet?'

'It's looking good for September next year, after the cricket season,' said Charlie, 'providing Henry can get the time off.'

'And where are you going to live?' asked Elspeth.

'Well, we have a family home in the West End, which is lying idle at present, because my elder brother, the duke, is recuperating from an operation and has removed himself to the family seat in Essex. When I broke the news to him about the forthcoming nuptials, he told me that Henry and I could take the place over, since he didn't see himself needing to make much use of it. He's getting on a bit, there's twenty-five years between us. I was a real afterthought. My parents thought their days of producing heirs were long over, but it seems they were wrong, because along I came.

'Now all this brings me to another item for the agenda. Tolstoy, my dearest and closest friend, would you do me the honour of being my best man?'

'Do you the honour? Do you the honour?' he repeated, to emphasise how he felt. 'It is you who honours me with such a wonderful invitation,' said Tolstoy with a broad grin. 'I should be deeply honoured and delighted to be your best man – well, provided Henrietta has no objection.' He glanced quizzically in her direction.

'As long as you keep your big feet off my hair, my veil and my bridal train, I should be delighted if you were to be Charlie's best man,' she said with a warm smile.

Tolstoy was deeply moved. He felt strangely tearful, yet wildly elated for his friend. A huge step was being taken. Whether it would be a step away from Charlie's old life and his old friends only time would tell. It was marvellous news though, and Henrietta certainly seemed better disposed towards him, compared with their first two meetings. This could only be good. Glasses were raised again, and contents drained. Tolstoy went over to the fridge, took out another bottle of champagne and uncorked it; Elspeth busied herself preparing the meal, and conversation moved gently on to other goings-on in the village and the surrounding area. 'Have you heard about Jo, the barmaid at the Snitcher's Head?' asked Tolstoy.

'No,' replied Charlie.

'Oh, she and Harry Stoke are an item,' chipped in Henrietta. 'In fact the talk in the village, according to my mother's cleaner, is that they are going to be married early next year.'

'Ah,' said Tolstoy, 'she sort of alluded to that when I was in the Snitcher's earlier today. In fact, Harry was there too, sitting discreetly at one end of the bar. And Jo did intimate that she hoped and believed that the relationship might turn more serious.'

Henrietta smiled. 'They make a good-looking couple. And they both have an amazing work ethic.'

'Yes they do,' agreed Tolstoy. 'At one point she had three or even four jobs a day, and I remember she told me she was saving up to leave the village and head up to London, and see what real life was like in a city. I did not try to put her right, but she was clearly one of those people who think that the grass is always greener elsewhere. And show me an idle gamekeeper. Harry seems to work all the hours and more than there are in a day.'

Charlie butted in, 'Well, if she is going to settle down and become Mrs Stoke, London is the last place she will be living. I don't think there's much call for gamekeepers or their wives in the West End or the Square Mile.'

While they had been chatting Elspeth had left the kitchen, but she now returned and took Tolstoy to one side. 'I've just tried to reach the colonel, but there was no answer and I didn't want to leave a message. I know he does enjoy a late snifter in the Snitcher's Head on the odd night, so on the off chance that tonight is one of those when he pops in to the pub, perhaps you could slip over with Charlie and Henrietta after we've finished dinner and have a quiet word with him. Would that be OK?'

'Yes. That's fine. We can head over there after I've helped clear up.'

The meal passed cheerily and noisily, with Tolstoy having to descend once more to the cellar in search of a couple more bottles. When all were replete, the table cleared and chairs pushed back, Henrietta decided that she would not go to the pub, but rather she would stay behind and give Elspeth a hand with the washing-up. However, Charlie and Tolstoy were instructed by Henrietta not to stay too long at the Snitcher's Head, no "one for the road" or similar nonsense, she warned. Tolstoy was reminded by Elspeth that he had a mission, so the pair promised that they would have no more than a couple of pints before returning to the Manor. Thus it was that they pulled on sweaters against the cold and crunched down the driveway to the gates of Stottenden Manor and the road beyond.

The bar was largely quiet. There were no more than perhaps a dozen people there, including Old Ned on his usual corner stool, nursing a cider, and, importantly for Tolstoy, the colonel was also numbered in the modest gathering. Tolstoy was disappointed not to see Kate among the other customers.

Charlie had insisted on buying the first round and after giving the order to Jo, including a pint of cider for Old Ned, he turned and called out, 'Evening, Andrew. Care for a refill?'

The colonel had been chatting with Harry Stoke, but after raising his hand in Tolstoy's direction, he turned back to his keeper briefly, said something, before making his way along the bar to the two of them.

'Good evening, Charlie, Tolstoy. Thank you for the kind offer. A pint of Fuggles would go down rather well.' And, after draining what little remained of his pint, he handed the glass to Jo for the refill.

'Well, Tolstoy, how are you settling into your new home?'

'Just fine, Andrew. Elspeth has been looking after me extremely well. She's a great cook and hasn't let me lift a finger as far as household chores go. However, I have been doing my bit for her by going into the cellar and rooting through some old trunks and suitcases, which she says Hubert had always meant to go through but never got around to doing it. They were tucked away in a distant, dusty and spider-infested corner. So I had to drag them out and get them under one of the bare lights to see if there was anything of interest.'

He paused long enough for the colonel, his curiosity piqued, to realise that Tolstoy had something of import to tell him, and was waiting for a nibble from him.

'Really? And did you find anything of interest?' he inquired, a smile playing gently at the corners of his mouth.

'Yes, but I'm sworn to secrecy until you and Miriam are able to come over to Stottenden Manor for drinks, either tomorrow, Friday, or sometime over the weekend. At which point we have something of interest to show you.'

'A mystery, eh? Well, I love a mystery, especially when, by the look on your face, it could well have a happy outcome.

All right. What time do you retire at the Manor, because either I or Miriam could ring you later to let you know when?'

'I'm usually in bed by midnight, Elspeth generally slips off around eleven. But tonight she is entertaining Henrietta Charles, while Charlie and I are indulging ourselves in a nightcap of Fuggles, so we should still be up and about. But failing that, you can always try us first thing in the morning. Elspeth is very much an early bird, she gets up at six most days. I am a little slower in surfacing, but I am still up and about by seven or seven-thirty. So you could give us a ring whenever. I'll leave it up to you and Miriam. But it is most important that you call in to the Manor at some point this weekend. I think you will appreciate the urgency once you know what it is that is so important. I can assure you it's most exciting. Elspeth and I can't wait to tell you, but it needs to be revealed in absolute privacy, and as you know, bars have ears.' Tolstoy winked theatrically and grinned. The colonel smiled.

'By the way, Andrew, I take it you have heard Harry Stokes' news?' Charlie cut in.

'Ah, the forthcoming nuptials with young Jo there,' he indicated the barmaid with a nod in her direction. 'Yes, I have and it is splendid news as far as Miriam and I are concerned. Ever since Harry arrived, Miriam, once she discovered he was single, has maintained it is a waste of a gorgeous man and has fretted about whether he would find someone suitable. But I must say, I think he has done rather well there. Jo is a singularly attractive young woman. They are a well-matched pair. And Miriam is pleased and relieved. The only sad aspect is that it means the cottage will fall empty again, because, as I understand it, they intend moving into Jo's cottage. That means we'll have lost a trustworthy tenant, who doubles up as a sort of security guard to us older folk. But never mind. I think it is more important for Harry to have someone with whom to share his life. And I cannot imagine a more suitable person than Jo. So they certainly have our blessing. What do you guys think?'

'Marvellous news,' said Charlie. 'That should also go a long way to keeping Harry in the village, and that will be good news for the cricket team and the Guns XI.'

'Quite,' said the colonel. 'Not to mention the benefit to the shoot. For some time now I've been looking to expand it, by renting shooting rights over the farmland adjacent to us, but on the north side. It's Brian Marlow's land, in all he has about 800 acres, but at the moment I'm just looking at shooting over around 250. However, he suggested why not shoot over all 800. That, though, would mean having to build probably another two release pens, which in turn would almost certainly entail having to employ an underkeeper for Harry. However, if we did use all of Brian's land it wouldn't cost us anything, because he has said that a gun in the syndicate for himself and his younger son Graham would be all we would have to pay him for rent. So it is tempting. And of course, if I took on another keeper that would mean our cottage would not remain vacant for long.'

Tolstoy moved up to the bar and caught Jo's eye, indicating three more pints to her. She duly began filling clean glasses. Ordinarily Tolstoy would have stopped her, and insisted that the ones they had could be re-used, but not this time, he felt it would appear too fussy.

'Ah, Tolstoy. Wicked man,' said the colonel, as Jo pushed a full glass across the bar to him. 'I promised Miriam I would be back by ten-thirty. It's ten-fifteen now and I am no longer young enough to knock back a pint in seconds. But thank you all the same. I shall not let it go to waste. Too good a pint for that.'

Charlie and Tolstoy duly received their pints and all three sipped, savouring the singular hoppy flavour of their favourite beer. Tolstoy was halfway down his pint when Charlie said, 'By the way, Andrew, Harry and Jo are not the only ones getting hitched in the not too distant future. I finally proposed to Henrietta last weekend. Then last night, after dinner with her parents I did the dutiful thing and asked her father for his daughter's hand in marriage. He agreed, gave us his blessing, her mother gave me a hug, so now all that is left is to fix a date. We're thinking tentatively of a September wedding, here in St Martin's.'

'Goodness gracious! The world's gone mad for marriage. Well, congratulations, Charlie, I have to say that Henrietta is quite some catch.'

Tolstoy stepped in. 'And so is Charlie.'

'Yes, yes, of course he is,' said the colonel, hurriedly correcting himself. 'I didn't mean that there was only one beneficiary in this union. Well, well! And presumably at some point he'll be able to add a title to anything else that he brings into Henrietta's life. I take it the ring is a fitting one, so to speak?'

'It resembles a highland cairn,' quipped Tolstoy. 'But one constructed from diamonds, rather than granite.' Charlie grinned.

'Well, once again my heartiest congratulations, Charlie,' said the colonel, glancing at his watch. 'Now, I'm afraid I must dash. If nothing else, I need to chat to Miriam about your drinks invitation and the mystery which is going to be uncovered when we drop in on you.' With that he drained his glass, replaced it on the bar and headed for the door.

'I suppose we ought to think of moving as well,' said Charlie.

'Yes,' agreed Tolstoy. 'We need to get back before the colonel rings. It wouldn't do to be still here when he does call.' They finished the last of their beer, said goodnight to Jo, Harry and Old Ned, and headed back to the Manor. There they found Elspeth and Henrietta sitting at the kitchen table, each nursing a balloon of brandy, their hands wrapped around each glass. The men were offered a late-night snifter. Charlie opted for a Scotch while Tolstoy declined any spirit, instead heading over to the table to see what wine remained, then they both joined the women, Tolstoy allowing Charlie to report on the meeting with the colonel.

'I must say he seemed very excited about it, even though he hasn't a clue what it is you two have unearthed,' said Charlie. 'And I must admit I'm getting quite excited about it. The suspense is wonderful.'

'Do you think he'll ring tonight?' asked Elspeth.

'Not sure. What do you reckon, Tolstoy?'

'Well, I did give him the option of trying us from quite early tomorrow morning. I suppose it depends on Miriam. She may think it is too late now to disturb us. Then again, she may get caught up in Andrew's excitement. I've no idea, really.'

'Perhaps we should have invited Andrew around tonight,' mused Elspeth. 'By the way, Tolstoy, I have invited Henrietta and Charlie, although he doesn't know it yet, to the great unveiling as well. So Charlie, you are to keep yourself free for the moment until we hear from Andrew. What other news do you have?' She looked from Tolstoy to Charlie.

The latter obliged saying, 'Only that Andrew is hoping to expand the shoot and possibly take on an underkeeper to help Harry with the increased workload.'

'How is he going to expand the shoot? I thought he was at an optimum size already. He would surely need more land, wouldn't he?' queried Elspeth.

'Ah, well, he is hoping to persuade his neighbour, Brian Marlow, to rent him a few hundred acres. And apparently Marlow is interested, to the extent that, if he decided to go ahead, he would not charge any rent, but rather would want a gun in the syndicate for himself and his younger son.'

'Gosh, that would make it a very large operation, wouldn't it?'

'I suppose so,' said Charlie. 'But I think he would probably set up a second syndicate to help to cover the capital outlay needed for the expansion. After all, he would need more birds, therefore more feed, more release pens, therefore more materials to construct them, and he might have to employ more than one extra full-time keeper as well. It will be something to ask him whenever he turns up this weekend.'

At that moment the phone rang. Elspeth got up to answer it. 'Oh, Andrew, hello.' A pause.

'No, no, you're not disturbing anyone. We're all sitting around the kitchen table with a nightcap, half-hoping you would call, and lo and behold, you have. When can you drop in for a drink?' Another pause. 'Tomorrow is perfect. The sooner, the better. Shall we say around six o'clock?' A pause again, then, 'Perfect. See you both then. Good night.'

Elspeth returned to the table. 'Good, that's settled. Andrew and Miriam will be arriving around six tomorrow. So Charlie, will you and Henrietta be able to join us? And do you think I should offer nibbles?'

'Yes,' said Henrietta. 'We should love to join you. And if you like I'll prepare a couple of plates of nibbles myself and bring them round. How would that be?'

'Oh that would be so kind. Thank you, Henrietta, that is a most welcome offer. Let me get a pen and paper and we can work out what each of us will do. We don't have to be too fussy. And I do not need to make too many. But it would seem inhospitable if there was nothing to offer when we are having a drink. And of course you and Charlie must stay on for a meal.'

Henrietta tried to refuse, but failed dismally. 'But Elspeth, we have just had a meal here tonight. We can't come again tomorrow as well. I think Charlie and I should treat you to a meal. After all, if you're preparing nibbles as well, you have very little time to sort out an evening meal for four people. How about trying the Vine in Goudhurst? It's building a good reputation for its food.'

'Yes,' said Charlie, endorsing his fiancée's suggestion. 'And what's more we will order a taxi for you.'

Elspeth looked at Tolstoy and raised one eyebrow questioningly. Tolstoy said, 'I think that's an excellent idea. It will also give us a set time to entertain Andrew and Miriam, so we will not be in danger of overdoing the preprandial drinks. After all, if they were to stay on for too long, we should probably feel obliged to invite them to stay for a meal as well, which would put a further burden on you.'

'All right,' conceded Elspeth. 'The Vine it is. And thank you. Now, I am ready for my bed, so let's sort out these canapés.'

Elspeth and Henrietta sat down and worked out a menu, while Tolstoy volunteered to wash up their glasses. Then Charlie and Henrietta, after saying they would book a table for eight-thirty at the Vine, took their leave, promising to be back shortly before six the following evening.

EIGHT

Tolstoy was slightly nervous. He was sitting at a table in the Snitcher's Head on his own with a woman. What's more, he had to ask her something and there was no one else to help him out. It was up to him, and him alone, to put the question to her. He took a sip of coffee and looked at Kate Harborne over the rim. She had taken the morning off work and had bumped into Tolstoy outside the village store. They both agreed it was a little too cold to stand around chatting, so at Kate's suggestion a coffee in the pub was decided as the ideal solution.

She pre-empted him by turning towards him with a quizzical expression. 'Before we go on, I have to ask you something. You weren't waiting outside the village shop hoping to "bump into" me, were you?'

'Good heavens, no,' protested Tolstoy. 'This meeting is pure chance. I was hoping to catch you in here this evening, or over the weekend, to ask you a favour. When you suggested coffee here I thought that now would be as good a time as any, that's all.

'I do have a question for you; it's to do with history. Would you, offhand, know how to get old documents authenticated? I was told you were a historian and that you used to work for a museum in their documents and manuscripts department, so I thought you might have contacts there, still.'

'I certainly have a few former colleagues and friends there with whom I stay in touch. We meet up from time to time for the odd lunch or evening drink. Why would you need me to get in touch with them?'

'I have uncovered some documents at Stottenden that I need to have authenticated, and dated if possible, and I have no idea how to go about doing that. I assume it involves forensics, but I don't have a clue whether any laboratory can do anything and everything, or whether it requires a specialist company. And I was also wondering about how expensive all that might be. So I hoped you might be able to help.'

'Well, I have a couple of good contacts at the forensic laboratory that we used, and from what you have said I should think they would be more help to you. I shall get in touch with one of them, Wayne, he's a really nice guy and very good at his job. He's the deputy forensic scientist at his company in North London. Do you have the documents with you?' She then answered her own question. 'No, of course you don't. You weren't expecting to see me. OK, when can you get the documents to me?

'I am around for the rest of the morning, but I do have to go to the shop this afternoon. And that's when I might be able to get in touch with Wayne, to see about fixing a date. I take it they are house deeds or something like that and that you need them authenticated sooner rather than later?' There was a faint query at the end of her statement. Tolstoy gave a nod, then said, 'Excellent. And thank you. This could be great news. Um, but the documents are not exactly deeds, well, not really, anyway, but I have to ask you to keep this absolutely secret for the time being. Only Elspeth, Charlie, Henrietta, me and now you, know of the existence of these documents, no one else. We have invited the colonel around to Stottenden this evening to show him the documents, because they may well relate to the Buttercup Field, and if so, they might well bring an end to the matter, and leave the Buttercup Field as it is, safe for the village.'

Kate's face took on a glow of excitement. 'Oh Tolstoy, that sounds wonderful. I promise I shall keep it secret. And I shall ask Wayne to treat it as a matter of urgency and confidentiality. Oh, I can't wait to see them and handle them, it's like handling history. It makes everything so much more real.'

'If you have time, why not come back to the Manor with me now?'

He looked at her hopefully. She leaned forward, lifted her coffee cup and took a last thoughtful sip, before replacing the cup and sitting back in her chair. Tolstoy couldn't help noticing a faint tinge of her delicate pink lipstick on the rim of the cup, which prompted him to glance at her full-lipped mouth. 'OK, let's go look at these documents now,' she said.

Ten minutes later Kate was on the verge of fulfilling her wish to see and handle the documents. She, Elspeth and Tolstoy were in the library, looking at the old brown legal envelope.

'I think, before you pull them out of the envelope, you ought to put on some gloves to handle the documents. Preferably cotton ones, to keep any acids or grease from your fingers and hands from getting onto the documents and causing possible damage. The older the documents, the more damage can be done.'

'Oh,' said Tolstoy, frustration in his voice, 'I don't possess any cotton gloves, in fact I don't have any gloves of any description.'

Elspeth came to his rescue. 'Don't worry, I have some cotton gloves. They probably won't fit you, but I am sure they would fit Kate. After all, she's the expert and so she should be the one to handle the documents from now on. I'll go and get them.'

'Sorry, when I found them in the cellar neither Elspeth nor I thought about putting on gloves. We just didn't consider the possibility of damaging them with our bare hands,' said a chastened Tolstoy. 'Don't worry too much. I am just being extra cautious. I'm sure that you won't have done them any harm,' said Kate consolingly. 'And it also depends on how old they are. The older they are the more prone they are to absorbing the oils from our skin and other secretions.'

'If the date that is written on them is accurate, then they are not far short of two hundred years old. Will that mean they will be OK?'

Hearing the anxiety in his voice, Kate reassured Tolstoy. 'Yes. There should be no problem.'

Elspeth returned with a pair of dove grey gloves and handed them to Kate. She pulled them on, then picked up the envelope and inserted her right hand, gently extracting the papers that lay within. She unfolded them, and after studying the plans, she read the letter, looked at the plans again then nodded her head.

'While I don't want to raise your hopes, I do think these are what they say they are and that they were drawn up when they say they were. I'm pretty certain Wayne will be able to authenticate these fairly quickly. The ink can be dated, so can the paper, and the handwriting and style of English can also be used to establish when the documents were created.

'In fact,' she glanced at her watch, 'I think I shall ring Wayne now. It's not yet lunchtime and anyway he has his lunch sitting at his desk. I will sort out a time when I can get the documents to him.' She pulled her phone from her pocket and began dialling. Tolstoy protested, telling her she could use the house phone, but she demurred and interrupted him by greeting her former colleague, who must have answered at his end on the first ring.

Kate moved away and slowly wandered towards the library door, all the while explaining what was needed. Then she paused. Tolstoy realised he had been holding his breath, letting it out with a soft woof when he heard Kate say, 'Oh, that would be brilliant. I'll meet you at Tunbridge Wells station and treat you to lunch. That's so kind of you. Look forward to seeing you tomorrow, OK, and thanks again, bye.'

She turned back to the expectant Elspeth and Tolstoy. 'Well, that's fantastic. Wayne has said he'd be happy to do it for a very modest fee, and a contribution to his travel expenses and any other incidental expenditure necessitated by the research. And, he can pick up the documents from me tomorrow. He has no idea how long it will take but he's certain, given the relative youth of the documents, that he'll have something to tell us by the middle of the week after next. Isn't that great?'

'It most certainly is,' said Elspeth. 'I thought it would be weeks if not months of arcane tests and examinations. This is really good news and so exciting.'

'I think it would be sensible then if you were to come round here for drinks this evening with the colonel and Miriam,' said Tolstoy. 'That means you could take them away with you after we have all finished looking at them. Is that going to be a problem? Otherwise I could always drop them in at your place later this evening or first thing tomorrow morning.'

'Thank you, and no, it's no problem, I'd be happy to call round this evening for a drink. I might not be able to make it at precisely six, because I have some stuff to sort out at the shop, and traffic on the way home can be dreadful on a Friday evening.'

'We'll excuse you being late,' said Elspeth, smiling. 'Good. That's settled then. Thinking about you transporting them home and then to Tunbridge Wells and remembering how careful we have had to be in handling the envelope and the documents, do we need to put the envelope into something else to prevent any 21st century contamination?'

'If you have any kind of file folder that should be good enough,' replied Kate.

'We have the very thing in the desk,' said Elspeth. Tolstoy turned to look. 'Third drawer down on the right, Tolstoy, there should be half a dozen of them. They are pastel-coloured cardboard ones.' Tolstoy withdrew a pale blue folder from the drawer and held it up for all to see. 'Will that be OK, Kate?' asked Elspeth.

'Perfect. Now I really do have to go. The earlier I get to the shop, the earlier I can leave this afternoon. See you both at or just after six.' Tolstoy showed Kate to the door, then returned to the library.

'This is so exciting,' said Elspeth. 'I can't wait to see the faces of the councillors, and especially Jack Bentley's, when we produce these documents.'

'Let's just hope they are the real thing and that Jack's collection is not,' said the ever-cautious Tolstoy. 'Well, I'm really looking forward to seeing Andrew and Miriam this evening. It'll be good to pass on this news. And I'm sure these,' she indicated the brown envelope, 'are the genuine article.'

'Well we're soon going to find out. We're so lucky to have someone with Kate's expertise and contacts for something like this. Now, do you need me to do any shopping? I can nip down to the village shop if you like.'

'No, I'm heading off to the supermarket shortly, once I've written out a comprehensive shopping list. They should have everything I need there. The village shop is my usual port of call, but I need more specialist things for the nibbles. It is so kind of Henrietta to volunteer to help out this evening with the canapés. What are you going to do now?'

'I think I'd better head back down to the cellar and tidy things up. I might even take the vacuum cleaner down there and get rid of some of that dust.'

'Right. I'll leave you to it. I thought we'd have soup for lunch. That OK with you?'

'Lovely, thanks Elspeth.'

'Right, I'll be leaving in a few minutes.'

Tolstoy headed for the cellar via the kitchen. Elspeth sat at the library desk and began to write out her shopping list. There was still a lot to do and time was running out. The colonel was punctual, pulling on the Victorian doorbell of Stottenden Manor on the stroke of six. He and Miriam were greeted by Tolstoy, who had managed to smarten himself up after a long hard afternoon in the bowels of the building, double-checking all the boxes, trunks and suitcases to ensure there was nothing more of import that had been overlooked. The dust had, for the large part, been vacuumed, he had even changed the old-fashioned lightbulb for a much brighter one that used a tenth of the electricity. He and Elspeth had made a brief tour of the cellar just prior to the colonel's and Miriam's arrival, and Elspeth had declared herself thrilled that such an unpleasant task had been carried out so well.

Once Tolstoy had taken their coats and hats and had hung them on pegs in the cloakroom off the cavernous hall of the Manor, he ushered them into the library, where logs blazed in the large fireplace, and Elspeth waited to greet them, along with Charlie and Henrietta, who had arrived earlier, bearing half a dozen plates and trays, each of which was laden with a different canapé, as Henrietta had promised.

The all-important envelope, whose contents had already been viewed by Charlie and Henrietta, lay on the antique partners' desk. Tolstoy eyed it as he entered the room, but said nothing. Elspeth offered the guests a drink, a gin and tonic for Miriam, a Scotch and soda for the colonel. Once all four had a drink Elspeth asked them to come over to the desk. Tolstoy then indicated for Elspeth to do the honours. She stepped up to the desk, pulled on her cotton gloves, picked up the envelope and removed its contents.

She spread out the documents on the desk and invited the colonel and his wife to have a look, warning them to try to avoid handling them if at all possible. Meanwhile Tolstoy explained where he had found them.

'Well, well,' said the colonel, straightening up after a couple of minutes, having studied them closely, 'if these are the real thing, then we have all the proof of ownership that we need.'

'As far as we can tell these are genuine,' said Elspeth. 'But Tolstoy chatted to Kate Harborne this morning and she's contacted a forensic chap she knows, who told her he's willing to take these and authenticate them and date them for us, which is wonderfully exciting. I'm certain they will be found to be the real thing and then this whole nonsense of the Buttercup Field can be laid to rest.'

The colonel looked astounded, but pleased. 'What an absolutely amazing find, and what a stroke of luck being able to have them authenticated like this. When is Kate's chap going to look at them?'

'She's meeting him tomorrow in Tunbridge Wells and he will take them back with him to London. Kate seems to think that we could have the result of the tests by the middle of the week after next, which would be fantastic. But even if it takes longer, very little is going to happen between now and the rescheduled hearing. By the way, when is that?'

'I still haven't heard. I think I'll contact them on Monday and remind them that we are running out of dates for this year. We're not too far from Christmas, and I'm certain most government departments will not be functioning at full throttle in the run-up to the festive season. Of course, if we get positive results from these authentication tests, then it would surely obviate the need for a hearing, which would be wonderful news for everyone. I'm sure no one is all that keen on taking part at this time of year, when there is so much else going on, what with Christmas shopping, arranging holidays, relatives coming to stay, or going off to visit members of the family.'

The doorbell sounded again. 'Oh, I expect that'll be Kate,' said Elspeth. 'Tolstoy, do you mind letting her in?'

Tolstoy could hardly wait. He shot out of the library and hauled the door open. It was indeed Kate. She was smiling. Tolstoy smiled back. 'Come in.'

'I'm sorry I'm so late. I got held up at the shop by a couple of phone calls and then the traffic was appalling.'

'You're not late, we've barely taken a sip of our first drink of the evening. Here, let me have your coat, I'll hang it up over there.' He indicated the cloakroom. 'Right, let's go into the library.' Once Kate had been handed a drink, the colonel quizzed her about whether they should be optimistic about the authentication of the documents. Kate was cautious, but encouraging. 'It's not quite my field, but having had a chance to study them this morning, and in good light, I think there is nothing to suggest they are forgeries, or at least, if they are, then they are 200-year-old forgeries. But I'm not the expert. That's Wayne's field, my forensic scientist friend. And he really is good. Also, when he says that he should have finished with the documents by the middle of the week after next, then that's when we can expect to have them back. He would never raise our hopes unless he was ninety-nine per cent certain that the investigation will not take any longer.'

'Well, that is excellent,' said the colonel. 'Hearing that has really fired me up to get on to the Home Office and sort out a date for this public inquiry, although I should be inclined to warn them that we might not need a hearing of any description.'

'Has Jack Bentley recovered from his heart problem?' asked Tolstoy. 'Only we heard that he was in the pub yesterday evening and apparently behaving like a dog with two tails.'

'Yes, I was told that as well,' said the colonel. 'But I wasn't able to hang around long enough to hear what had made him so upbeat.'

So while Tolstoy did the rounds, refilling glasses, Charlie repeated his news of the previous evening, that Bentley had also announced the discovery of some documents proving ownership of the Buttercup Field.

At this the colonel raised an eyebrow. 'So where does that leave these documents, then?' He indicated the documents that lay in front of them all.

'We think, on the side of right,' said Elspeth, firmly. 'Once these documents have been proved to be genuine, we would then be in a position to challenge Jack Bentley to have his set of papers authenticated, *independently*,' she stressed the last word.

'Hmm, this could make for some interesting times ahead,' said the colonel. 'I must say I should like to be there when old Jack hears about these documents. It will probably have him spluttering into one of his late-landed cognacs. I wonder if his documents were drawn up around the same time. That would create a few problems for everyone. Well, no point in speculating. We shall all soon know, one way or the other. I take it someone, one of you presumably, will let me know the upshot of the authentication of these documents when you hear from Kate?'

'Of course,' said Elspeth. 'I shall ring you the second we find out.'

'And if it's good news,' suggested Miriam, 'perhaps we could organise some sort of celebration to follow at a later date. Maybe in the Snitcher's Head?'

'Or here,' countered Elspeth. 'After all, the documents belong here, and so will the land, if they are genuine pieces of paper.'

'Yes, you're right. It would be far more appropriate to hold any sort of celebration here at Stottenden Manor,' conceded Miriam.

The colonel chipped in. 'Well, I think it's better not to get too far ahead of ourselves, after all we still don't know if the documents are genuine. But I agree, some sort of village celebration here would be perfect.' Miriam brought the conversation back to more mundane matters. 'I have to say these canapés are absolutely wonderful. They really are terribly good. I'm terrible at making this sort of thing. I always struggle with anything foreign or fancy.'

'We have Henrietta to thank for these deliciously tasty morsels,' said Elspeth, dismissing her own contribution to the evening's nibbles. 'This wonderful young woman has clearly given up most of her day off to produce these stunning mouthfuls.' More canapés were passed around, more sips of drink taken, and more casual chitchat was enjoyed. Until finally, with Elspeth beginning to glance with increasing frequency at her watch, the colonel and his wife got the message that it was time to go. Tolstoy went out to the cloakroom and gathered up their coats and hats, before handing them out. Finally, the pair of them were ready to brave the chilly evening and they departed.

Tolstoy returned to the library and asked Kate if she felt like joining them at the Vine, but, after thanking him for the invitation, she said she had other things on and so would have to give it a miss, but wished them *bon appétit*. She then got up from her chair, made her way over to the desk and picked up the envelope, now safely in its folder, tucked it under her left arm and made her way towards the library door. Tolstoy leaped to his feet and took her by the arm to steer her into the hall. 'Thank you so much for sorting this out, and so quickly and efficiently, Kate. I really appreciate it. As Elspeth said earlier, I imagined the authentication taking ages. As it is, we may well know the fate of the Buttercup Field by this time next week. It's fantastic of you to help out in this way.'

'I'll let you know the moment Wayne has any news. In fact, I shall get him to call me when he gets himself and the documents safely back to his place tomorrow. And you're right, it really is exciting.' Tolstoy helped her on with her coat and, with a final glance and smile at Tolstoy, she slipped out of the front door and was quickly lost to the darkness of the November evening.

Tolstoy remained at the open door for a few seconds, wondering if he should have arranged to see Kate over the weekend, but he just could not pluck up the courage to ask her out, as much as he wanted to. He had hoped she would agree to join them at the Vine, but it was too short notice for her, he appreciated, and after all, she did have a life of her own to lead. Slowly he closed the door and returned to the library.

NINE

Late the following morning Tolstoy wandered down to the cricket field. He had been feeling guilty for some weeks because he had been putting off the visit, and he knew he had to check things over and see what needed to be done to the outfield, the pitch and the pavilion, not to mention checking on the equipment and finding out what needed servicing and repairing. He had telephoned Bert Bryson, a cricket club member, who had also worked for the borough council as a grass cutter, with responsibilities for maintaining grass verges on all the roadsides in the area, clearing ditches on aforementioned roadsides, keeping the local cemetery tidy and, when it was called for, digging graves. He had been retired for some years, but he had now adopted the mantle of Stottenden CC's head groundsman. And a couple of days earlier he had agreed to meet Tolstoy at the pavilion, to discuss what needed to be done over the winter.

Bert was a former player, a purveyor of handy leg spin and, in his day, an explosive and often match-winning batter. Sadly, his knees and a hip had rendered him incapable of playing a useful part in the village team, and so he had retired some dozen years earlier, but with the promise that he would take over the duties of preparing the outfield and pitch, and this he had done, to great acclaim, it had to be said. He had renovated the square, using Ongar loam. There was not a weed to be seen on the outfield, and despite the fact that he would have preferred a motorised roller, Bert had somehow managed, with the help of the heavy old manual roller, to iron out many of the irritating little ridges and kinks on both the square and the outfield that had bamboozled cricketers for years, and sent cricket balls flying over their heads, or whizzing unexpectedly to one side or the other of a fielder's desperately flailing, outstretched hands. Bert was reliable, too. He was often to be seen during the winter months pottering about, prodding this, poking that, assessing what, if anything, needed to be done. He was already at the pavilion when Tolstoy arrived. Bert must have been examining something at the rear of the building, because, as Tolstoy approached from the Manor, the old groundsman emerged from behind the building.

He waited until Tolstoy was within hearing distance before greeting him. Tolstoy responded and by then was close enough to shake hands.

'Bert, I'm so sorry that I haven't had a chat with you sooner,' said Tolstoy.

'That's all right, sir. No need to fret. Everything is under control 'ere.'

'I'm glad to hear it, but I'm sure there are still things that need seeing to. I've had a few thoughts myself, but I wanted to hear what you have to say first. And please, call me Tolstoy, everyone does. I find "sir" a bit too daunting.'

'Right oh, uh… Tolstoy. Well, I think we need a new shed to keep the equipment in. That lean-to at the back of the pavilion is about ready to drop. All it'll take is a puff of wind and down she'll come. So what I reckoned was maybe, putting up a shed, a decent-sized one, nearer the entrance from the Manor. We'd need power, light and water there, but it doesn't 'ave to cost the earth.'

'Sounds good to me,' said Tolstoy. 'Can I leave it to you to choose the shed? And do you know any electricians and plumbers who could do the necessary for water, and power?'

'Yes, you can leave all that to me,' said Bert, surprised that his suggestion had met with no resistance whatsoever. Not like with the old man. Old de Groot would have argued the toss, kicked up a bit of a fuss, before eventually insisting on finding the cheapest this or that. He never, ever considered anything new. So Bert thought he'd try his luck a little further, adding, 'Also, the Road End sight screen needs some new wheels. Well actually, it wants rebuilding altogether. The base is held together with paint.'

'Yes, I noticed that during the summer,' said Tolstoy. 'Is there a good carpenter in the village who could build two new sight screens, do you think?'

'Hmm, I'll think on that. There's a chap in Goudhurst who might be able to take on the job, but it could turn out to be pricey.'

'Well, we'll see what sort of a price we'd have to pay for a ready-made one and compare it with one that is made specifically to our specifications. I'll look into that. Now, I think we could do with upgrading the spectators' toilets, and you have actually been helpful there with your thoughts on a new shed, because I think it would be feasible to erect toilets at the rear of the pavilion. What do you reckon?'

Flattered to be consulted in this way, old Bert thumbed off his flat cap and ran a thoughtful finger through his sparse hair, before saying, 'Is that toilets for the players as well then?'

'No. The changing room facilities are pretty good. But the ramshackle affair on the far side of the pavilion does need a makeover or pulling down. I think the latter. We could then look into putting up some sort of building in that general area, with the drainage system – maybe instal one of those sewage treatment plants, or a septic tank – perhaps twenty-five yards or so beyond the pavilion, on the side furthest from the road. What do you think?'

'Well, it all sounds like a lot of money to me. When do you propose to put up the new toilets?'

'I think early spring, when the weather is better for working outdoors.'

'Well, I can't say as it isn't overdue. Long overdue. I just 'ope the new toilets last as long as the old 'uns though, because these days nothing seems to last as long, does it?'

Tolstoy agreed. Then he said, 'Just a couple more things. I've been thinking of getting a proper scorebox, you know, covered, with enough seating room for the two scorers and a couple of scoreboard operators. Any thoughts?'

'Well, Tolstoy, that 'ould make for a classy club ground and no mistake. But again, cost?'

'This will come out of my pocket. After all, I'm the numbers man for the club. I would like to present it to Stottenden in memory of Hubert. I haven't mentioned this idea to anyone, especially not Mrs de Groot, because the idea only just came to me. So mum's the word, but perhaps you could help research where we might obtain something like that?'

'I'd be delighted, Tolstoy, and I think that's a grand way to remember Mr de Groot, and indeed all 'is family.'

'Good,' said Tolstoy, 'that's settled then. Now, I think we need a proper roller. A ride-on one of around maybe, half or three-quarters of a ton. And also we need to look at the mowers. I've watched the ground staff at the county grounds and they use manual cylinder mowers for the pitch. We ought to follow that example. And I do think we could do better with a decent triple gang cylinder mower for the outfield, something like an Allen mower, although that would have to be second-hand, and one for which we could still obtain spare parts. The old mower we have, with just the one cutting cylinder, is nowhere near as efficient as an Allen would be. I think our present mower dates back to the 1940s, or even earlier, and I don't think spares are that easy to get hold of. Have you any thoughts on where we might look?'

'Well, an Allen triple gang would be ideal, manageable, and extremely efficient, but even second 'and they don't come cheap, and finding a second 'and one could take quite a while. But councils are always auctioning plant and machinery and vehicles. It might be worth calling the borough council and seeing if they have anything going. It might be worth trying a plant hire company, although I should imagine anything from a hire company would 'ave been flogged to blazes. Or you could go to the auction at Paddock Wood. They often have those government surplus auctions there, where you can buy old police cars, Royal Mail vans and suchlike.'

'What an excellent idea, thanks Bert, I shall certainly do that. Maybe that's where we could pick up a roller as well?'

'Yes, although the bigger cricket clubs and sports grounds may well 'ave something like a roller that they want to get shot of.'

'How are you on the mechanics of mowers and rollers?'

'Fine. Before I became a groundsman I did an apprenticeship at an agricultural and 'orticultural engineers, and they taught me everything I know. I can service anything, two-stroke, four-stroke, chain saws, mowers, chippers, stump grinders, pretty well anything. They trained me well. Unfortunately they hit a lean spell and, not long after finishing my indentures, they had to put me out to grass, so to speak.' Bert paused and smiled at his little joke. 'But full credit to 'em, one of the directors 'eard about the council's scheme for training up groundstaff, put me on to it, told me to tell the council I could carry out basic maintenance on whatever machine I was put in charge of and the rest is 'istory.'

This potted autobiography made Tolstoy realise that Bert had been underused throughout his time with the cricket club. They had sent the machines away for servicing and repairs, he knew that because he had seen the numerous invoices from various engineering companies. He decided that Bert's shed could and should be a lot larger, big enough to house the sort of equipment he would need to maintain the cricket club's machinery. This was going to call for a longer session than he had time for today, but he would make sure he sat down with Bert sooner rather than later to work out what and how much.

'Would you be prepared to service and repair, within reason, our equipment?' asked Tolstoy.

'Yes, I dare say I could do that. It'd make things a lot cheaper for the club, for a start.'

'I want to make it clear that the club would pay you for all repair work and servicing that you carried out. As long as it will save the club some cash, and as long as you are happy to undertake the basic stuff.'

'I think we're going to need to talk a little further about these matters,' said Tolstoy. 'How about we meet here next Saturday, same time. By then I should have a better idea of what we can afford, and you will be able to track down items that you think we should have. And that must include the pricing and sizing of sheds, although I think you'll agree, we should be looking at something a little more ambitious than a large garden shed. I think we ought to have a building that will allow you to set up a work bench and store the tools you'll need, and all that sort of thing.'

'OK. Next Saturday's fine by me. Eleven-thirty again?'

'Yes. Right, I'm off to the Snitcher's Head.'

'Ah, so am I. I'm meeting Old Ned there for a pint. We always 'as a pint of a Saturday morning.'

'Well, we may as well go over there together.'

The pair set off across the cricket field, passed into the Buttercup Field, straight across that to the gate that led directly onto the road. At which point Bert halted.

''Ello, then, what's all this?' He crouched down by the large gatepost to which the gate was hinged. 'Looks like someone's dug up the gatepost and moved it, either in or out, I can't tell.' Bert looked up at Tolstoy. ''Ave a quick look at t'other post see if any diggin' has gone on there,' he instructed. 'If this post 'as been moved then t'other un 'as to 'ave been moved as well, unless the gate's new and is a different size from the original.'

'Nothing has been disturbed on this side,' Tolstoy reported. 'And the gate is the original one, I recognise some of the sets of initials carved into the top bar.'

'Ah, I expect if you looks 'ard enough you'll find mine and Ned's and a few others,' said Bert with a grin. He turned back to the post. 'Now I wonder what's been going on 'ere. It's a puzzle, that's what it is. And what's stranger, is that I don't recall seeing anyone working away at this, not in the last few days at any rate.'

He hauled himself to his feet, and after closing the gate, he and Tolstoy made their way across the road to the pub. Tolstoy did the honours, buying Bert, Old Ned and himself pints of bitter and cider. Then Tolstoy moved away from the bar and sought out a table. He sat down, stretched out his legs, took a long first pull at his beer, then, replacing the glass, he let out a long sigh. He reflected on the conversation with Bert and felt that the cricket club could only benefit from the old fellow's expertise. Maybe they could find a willing apprentice among the club's younger members, who could be trained by Bert in the art of groundsmanship and agricultural mechanics. A pipe dream, he was sure, but it would be worth sounding out a few of the senior members of the club, who might just have an idea or two on that front. Perhaps even had a son, daughter or a grandchild who might be interested in helping out. Nothing like starting them early. Not that Bert was on his last legs or anything, but he might appreciate the help during the bleak winter days, and he would certainly enjoy the company. It was something to consider.

He reached for his glass again and took a more modest sip, savouring it this time.

'Hah, Warren Pearce. The very man.' It was a plummy voice. Not one that Tolstoy thankfully had had to listen to too often, although that might be about to change.

He swivelled around and looked up at the figure of Jack Bentley. 'Good morning, Jack. Why would I be the very man? The very man for what?'

'The very man I want to speak to. Mind if I join you?' Bentley had already begun to lower his ample backside onto the chair to Tolstoy's right.

Tolstoy was peeved. He had been hoping to bump into Kate at some point, preferably here in the Snitcher's Head, and he did not want anyone else to monopolise him in case it put Kate off coming over to speak to him.

'I don't know if you've heard,' Bentley continued, 'but a couple of my farm workers came up with something a couple of days ago.'

'Oh?' said Tolstoy. 'What was that?'

'A box, containing some old documents.'

'Really?'

'Yes.'

Tolstoy waited, not wishing to give Bentley the satisfaction of having him ask about the significance of the documents. 'They confirm what I had suspected all along, that Hubert's grandfather Cornelis made a gift of the Buttercup Field to the parish council, for the use, and the betterment, of the village and its inhabitants, which I think you will agree would embrace a residential building project with affordable homes that would help to keep younger villagers in Stottenden.'

'Cornelis, you say? Is it dated?'

'Yes, 1895, so getting on for a hundred and twenty-five years or so ago.'

'And what do you propose doing with these documents?'

'Well, they should bring to an end all this nonsense about the Buttercup Field and preventing the proposed housing development from going ahead. I shall be making a presentation to the parish council at a meeting a week next Thursday.'

'But how do you know that the documents are genuine?' asked Tolstoy. 'For a start, where were they found? And by whom?'

'My lads found them by the roadside gate into the Buttercup Field.'

'How did they know to look there?'

'They weren't looking for the documents there, the post had worked loose and so I told them to reset it. When they were digging down they hit something hard, thought it was a stone, took a crowbar to it and up popped this wooden box. The crowbar had smashed the lid but, fortunately, had not damaged the contents, which meant I was able to read the declaration by Cornelis de Groot. There'll be no need for a public inquiry. Once the council has seen this they'll be able to give the go-ahead and building will be able to get under way within a month or six weeks. This is great news.'

Tolstoy was torn. He wanted to blurt out that his set of papers was older and was more likely to be genuine. At the same time he did not want Jack Bentley to know about what had come to light in the cellars of Stottenden Manor, not until he knew they were genuine. But he wanted to rattle the multi-millionaire "gentleman" farmer, if for no other reason than that he disliked the man and his upper class pretensions.

'I think that you may find the authenticity of the documents being challenged,' Tolstoy ventured. 'I doubt if any of the protestors, or perhaps I should say protectors, of the Buttercup Field are just going to accept these documents and what they say, not after all the trouble they have gone to in order to ensure that no building is going to take place in the field.'

'I fear you are clutching at straws,' said Bentley, barely disguising the sneer in his voice. 'I know you are on the protest committee. You are just a poor loser. You can't accept irrefutable evidence that your protests are now about to be rendered meaningless. Why not come along to the meeting on Thursday week? You can even get a close-up of the documents, you and the whole of your misguided committee.'

With that Bentley got to his feet, pushed back his chair and made his way to the end of the bar furthest from Tolstoy, where he joined a conversation with two of his workers. Tolstoy realised he had not asked after Jack Bentley's health. Still, did he really care? No, Tolstoy decided. He couldn't give a fig. He shrugged and returned to his contemplations and plans for the cricket ground. There was something really rather pleasing and reassuring about planning the future of something as worthwhile as the cricket club and its ground. He was glad that he had decided to involve Bert in everything. The old boy was switched on and Tolstoy felt sure that it would benefit the club if Bert's expertise were harnessed from the outset. And, although Bert might worry a little about the costs, in fact Hubert had been more than a little prudent with his spending, and Tolstoy knew there were ample funds to accomplish what he and Bert had discussed that morning. In truth, they could probably afford a new roller and a new mower or two. But Tolstoy, while wanting to get the best that could be afforded, still had a prudent streak of his own governing him, and he did enjoy coming across a second-hand bargain every now and again.

He reached for his glass, and found to his surprise that he had emptied it during his musings. He rose and went over to the bar to order another. Jo was serving at the far end, another big round being paid for by Jack Bentley, by the looks of it. Tolstoy waited, glancing around the pub, which had filled quite considerably. Just then he felt a tap on his shoulder and the voice of Kate Harborne intruded. 'Afternoon, Tolstoy. Mine's a dry white wine, please.'

He was smiling even as he turned to face her. 'Kate, I didn't expect to see you. I thought you'd be having a drink with your old colleague in Tunbridge Wells.'

'I've been there and returned. Wayne had to come down a lot earlier than he had originally intended, which meant I had to meet his train three hours earlier. We had a coffee, I handed him the documents and then he went back to London. I made sure that the assistants were coping in the shop, then thought I'd drop by here to see if you were around, so that I could let you know that Wayne had the documents. And I can tell you that he had a quick glance at them and said he was sure they are the real deal, but he will conduct a number of tests, which he assures me will establish the authenticity of the documents, or not, and he is confident he can complete everything, at the latest, by a week on Wednesday.'

Tolstoy was on the point of responding to Kate's news when Jo called to him, 'Were you looking for a refill, Tolstoy?' He turned, answered in the affirmative, and added Kate's drink to complete his order. 'Coming up,' said Jo.

'The timing looks perfect,' said Tolstoy. 'Jack Bentley had a quick chat with me a little earlier and said he would be presenting his documents to the council at their next meeting a week on Thursday, and he invited the whole of the campaign committee to sit in on the meeting, so confident is he that he has got this thing wrapped up.'

'Did you tell him about the documents you found?' asked Kate.

'No. Partly because I want to surprise him with them at that meeting, and partly because I am a naturally prudent person and I wouldn't want to tempt providence by claiming they were genuine, when they might well turn out to be forgeries themselves. Although who would have forged them, and why, and when, I have no idea. By the way, what are the arrangements between you and Wayne for the return of the documents?'

'He's hoping to be able to bring them down to Tunbridge Wells again, but on a very early train. He needs to be back in London by mid-morning for an important meeting.'

'Would it be easier if I met him?' asked Tolstoy. 'After all, the documents are to do with me.'

'That's very kind of you, Tolstoy, but I know what Wayne looks like, and he me. And anyway I need to be in Tunbridge Wells on that day, to open the shop. But,' she went on, after seeing a slight look of disappointment flit across Tolstoy's face, 'you could always come with me. Then you'd be able to meet Wayne, and we could have a breakfast together somewhere, either before meeting Wayne, or after.'

'Now that sounds like a plan. OK, I'll accompany you. Where shall we have breakfast? I don't know any places in Tunbridge Wells, except the obvious ones, the hotels.'

'Leave that to me,' said Kate. 'Obviously we'll have to go in my car, unless you've passed your test and I haven't heard about it.'

Tolstoy looked at her sheepishly. 'Have you had any driving lessons yet?' she asked.

'I've rather let all that slide,' he confessed. 'But I have promised Elspeth that I will start lessons when all this Buttercup Field hoo-hah is out of the way.'

'We'll fix a time for me to pick you up when I know precisely the day and time of Wayne's return. And I shall taxi you home again.'

'Oh there's no need for that. I can catch a train.'

'Well, we'll see.'

'If he can bring his invoice I could have some ready cash to pay him. Although I'd probably need a rough idea of how much cash he needs for expenses and his fee. Or if he prefers I could make it a cheque. If he could let you know then you could tell me.'

Tolstoy glanced over Kate's left shoulder to the corner of the bar occupied by Old Ned and Bert, as well as the two farm hands who worked for Jack Bentley. The conversation of the four men appeared to be getting heated. Abruptly the farm hands thumped their empty glasses onto the bar, turned and stalked out of the pub, leaving Old Ned and Bert chuckling.

While he had been observing the altercation, if that is what it was, Kate had been talking. Tolstoy refocused on her. 'I'm sorry, I didn't catch that, could you tell me again, please?'

Kate shook her head then began again. 'I was simply saying that breakfast the week after next will be our first date.'

Tolstoy stared open-eyed and open-mouthed at her. 'First date?'

'Yes. Except, of course, I know that it isn't our first date. It isn't really a date at all, it's just a necessity. A means to pass time while we wait for Wayne, or a chance to sit back and digest whatever news Wayne has for us about the documents.'

Tolstoy felt, simultaneously, a pang of guilt and of fear. Now was his chance to invite her out. He was petrified, but not so much that he was struck dumb. 'Um, what are you doing tonight?' he asked tentatively.

'Why? Are you thinking of asking me out? Oh, Tolstoy. I had been planning on vegging out in front of the telly. But if you're inviting me out, then the telly can stay off, and I can put my glad rags on.'

The red-faced Tolstoy was alarmed. Kate's voice had surely carried to the bar. He looked across, and sure enough Jo was smiling at him.

'Um, well, not exactly. No... I mean, yes. The problem is that I can't drive, so I was sort of thinking locally.'

'Like here, at the Snitcher's Head?' asked Kate.

'Well no. I mean I could arrange a taxi and we could go into Goudhurst, or Matfield, you know, the Vine or the Poet? They are getting praised to the heavens. We could also go to the Star and Eagle.'

'Well if we're going locally I could drive.'

'No.' Tolstoy frowned at Kate's suggestion. 'That would mean you couldn't have a drink, and I don't want to drink on my own.'

'A couple of glasses wouldn't hurt.'

'They might not hurt you, but what if you had an accident? What if it was someone walking home in the dark? Or you could run into a deer, heaven knows there are plenty of those about in this area, especially at night. Then the couple of drinks might be argued to have hurt that person or that deer. No. We'll go by taxi.' Tolstoy surprised himself by the firm tone he had adopted, but he knew he meant it. And he really did want to share a bottle of fizz with Kate, and get gently merry with her.

Kate smiled. 'OK. Taxi. Let's go to the Poet in Matfield. But make sure that the taxi does not come back to the Poet to pick us up too early. I want our first date to be a memorable one, and that means it has to be a lengthy one.'

'No problem. I shall order it for seven at the Manor and we'll pick you up at about five past, OK?'

She nodded and smiled again. Tolstoy's face also creased into a grin. He had done it. He had actually asked Kate out and she had accepted. Wonderful. He felt just wonderful. Liberated from some subconscious shackles that had bound themselves around him all these years.

He did wonder what Elspeth might say. And Charlie. He'd pull Tolstoy's leg for sure when he found out. Again he glanced over to the bar and Jo was still grinning broadly. She'd obviously heard every word. Well, he thought, so what? He was looking forward to finding out about Kate over a decent meal and good bottle of wine or two this evening.

Once again Kate broke into his musings. 'If we're going out tonight, then I need to get a move on, I need to help the girls cash up at the shop. Thankfully we close at five-thirty so I should have plenty of time to shower and change. But I'll have to leave now.' Tolstoy nodded as she stood up, then he practically fell off his chair as she leaned over and kissed him on the forehead. He blushed furiously. Kate just grinned and said, in a loud voice, 'See you this evening, Tolstoy,' and with that she was gone. Thankfully only Jo seemed to have witnessed that last exchange, and she applauded him silently before moving away to serve a customer. Tolstoy decided to head home and break his news to Elspeth. He hoped she'd approve of his choice.

TEN

Tolstoy had assured Elspeth that the documents were by now safely in London, and who knew, perhaps even undergoing testing right then. This conversation naturally led onto the subject of Kate, and Tolstoy, for some reason feeling slightly apprehensive, tentatively informed her of his dinner date that evening.

'Darling Tolstoy, that is the best news I have heard all year. It's even better than the discovery of the documents. I am thrilled for you. She is a wonderful young woman and perfect for you, as you are, of course, perfect for her. I am truly pleased. She is precisely the sort of woman that Hubert had wanted you to meet. I don't want to get ahead of myself, but I do hope things work out well tonight and all the other times you take her out on subsequent dates. Where are you taking her, again?'

Tolstoy told her, explained his promise to Kate to start driving lessons when everything was sorted about the Buttercup Field, and added that he was going to order a taxi for that evening.

'Oh don't be silly, Tolstoy. I'm more than happy to take you there and pick you up.'

But Tolstoy insisted that Elspeth should not find herself tied to an arrangement such as this. 'After all, we have no idea how long we shall be there.'

'And you would probably feel rushed whatever time I came to pick you up,' finished Elspeth perspicaciously. 'You're right. But if the taxi lets you down when you are ready to leave, you can just ring me. I shan't go to bed before you get home, I can assure you.' Before leaving the pub earlier, Tolstoy had gone over to Bert to thank him again for his time and his thoughts, and to reassure the groundsman that money was not going to be a problem when it came to acquiring mowers and a roller. Bert nodded his gratitude for Tolstoy's kind words and courtesy, then asked, 'You be going to the council meeting week after next?'

At Tolstoy's nod, he carried on, 'I'll be there too. Wouldn't miss it. It might be after Bonfire Night, but there's going to be fireworks that night, for sure, and something very interesting that involves the cricket club, the Manor and indeed the 'ole village.'

Tolstoy thought Bert was referring to the announcement of the documentary proof held by Jack Bentley and thought that maybe Bert supported the wealthy farmer-cum-speculator. But not a bit of it. 'You just make sure you're there,' said Bert. 'You'll regret it if you miss it.' He touched his nose and smiled conspiratorially, before repeating, 'Won't say no more. Can't say no more. But you mark my words. There's going to be fireworks that night, that's for sure.'

The statement had fired Tolstoy's curiosity, but he decided there was little point in pressing Bert. Maybe he could get the old man to tell him when they met up the following Saturday to compare notes about developments for the cricket ground. He intended visiting a couple of local companies that supplied agricultural and horticultural equipment to get some idea of what there was and what would be best suited to the needs of the cricket club. One place was walkable from the Manor, the other was in Paddock Wood, so he could take a train there. That was the one to visit first, then, on returning, instead of making the walk back up the hill to the village, he could go in the opposite direction, cross the main road and head down into the small industrial estate half a mile from the station, where the other place was situated.

Over lunch with Elspeth she inquired what his movements would be that afternoon and Tolstoy explained his planned window shopping expedition.

'But aren't they closed on a Saturday afternoon?' she asked.

'No. I checked with Bert. They are just about the only two in the county who stay open until five. But they do close on a Sunday.'

'Would you like me to drive you to them?' Elspeth asked.

'No, I'm looking forward to the walk and the train journey. I impose upon you too much for ferrying me around as it is. I really will organise a whole string of driving lessons very shortly, I'm just trying to get all this Buttercup Field stuff out of the way first. But I will aim to fix a date for my test as well, so that I have a deadline to meet. It is probably unrealistic of me, but maybe I could set a target of passing it before Christmas.'

'Don't put yourself under that sort of pressure,' said Elspeth. 'I doubt whether you would be able to book your test date that soon. I'm sure there is quite a long waiting list. But do get on and book some lessons. Perhaps starting the day after the council meeting, when, I'm sure, everything will have finally been sorted. You could see if Ken Pitcher would be able to take you on. He's an ex-army driving instructor and from what I've been told he has a very good reputation, and a record for getting many of his pupils through first time.'

Once the lunch things had been cleared away Tolstoy pulled on his quilted jacket, slung his small rucksack on one shoulder, bade Elspeth goodbye and set off for the station. It was an overcast day, but not unpleasant. No rain was forecast, and he was able to enjoy the views across the Weald. On leaving the Manor, the road on his left was flanked by the Buttercup Field, which ran for almost 150 yards, before it ended at a belt of trees. Then came a field, belonging to Jack Bentley, that generally was given over to cereal crops, and it looked as if it might have been sown with winter barley, or wheat. About halfway along this field the road began to descend. A seemingly gentle gradient, but, as Tolstoy knew, deceptively steep when approaching from the opposite direction. There was a large, rather grand-looking driveway on the left which led to the Bentley house, a modern, neo-Georgian monstrosity. A further three hundred yards below this was the entrance to Jack Bentley's farmyard, with an oast and two barns, set well back from the road. Another, smaller field followed, then the road levelled out and shortly after that Tolstoy was turning left into the station approach. He used the ticket machine, then stood patiently, waiting for the train. Surprisingly it was on time. Tolstoy had only had to wait a couple of minutes, before it appeared around the bend, belching white steam and grey smoke. The smell was heavenly. Tolstoy got in and moved down the corridor to an empty compartment where he took a seat facing the engine. He leaned forward in his seat and, despite the time of year, lowered the window, to ensure that the wonderful train smells filled the compartment, and then settled back for the twenty-five-minute journey into Paddock Wood through some of the most charming countryside in Kent.

It was dark by the time Tolstoy began the walk back up to the village from the station. His rucksack bulged with brochures and price lists. The Paddock Wood place dealt only with new plant and machinery. He had collected the available literature, but felt sure there was nothing there that really suited his needs. The local place, in contrast, had a large second-hand stock, but what made it even better was that it was part of a nationwide network of similar dealers with an extensive holding of used plant and machinery. It also had brand new stock. Again Tolstoy left there with a sizeable collection of brochures, but with an added incentive for sticking to the local engineering firm, because once they learned it was for Stottenden cricket club, they said that they would do a discount on the purchase of new or second-hand stock; further, they said servicing could be carried out on-site, rather than Tolstoy having to arrange transport for the mowers or rollers. This appealed greatly to the thrifty side of his nature, although he was mindful of Bert's expertise in this area, but still, it would do no harm to let them do the odd bit of servicing, provided it didn't cost the earth. Anyway, there might be jobs that Bert could not undertake. Tolstoy was buoyed up, and all in all he felt rather pleased with himself at having made the decision to do some window shopping for the equipment, because he had been able to come up with informed ideas, now that he had seen the machinery in the flesh, so to speak. As he toiled back up the hill towards Stottenden on this dark, damp, late afternoon in November, he was looking forward to having a long leisurely shower and getting ready to go out. To go out, he repeated to himself, with Kate Harborne. He was very nervous, but now also excited at the prospect. It was after five o'clock when he finally arrived at the front door of the Manor – his manor, his home, he reminded himself. He let himself in, moved into the cloakroom annexe, shrugged off his rucksack, hung his overcoat on a peg, then lugged the brochure-laden bag into the warmth of the living room, where he hoped to find Elspeth. She was nowhere to be seen, much to his disappointment, but nevertheless, he felt sure he wouldn't have to wait long before she appeared. *Meanwhile*, he thought, *I shall read these brochures more closely*. He had waded through about half of them before Elspeth entered the large room. 'Oh. Tolstoy, you're back,' she exclaimed. 'Would you like a cup of tea?'

'Oh yes, please,' he said. 'That would be wonderful. It's grown really quite chilly out.'

'Yes, it has. That's why I have closed all the ground floor shutters. They may be good for security, but they are also very effective forms of insulation. Right, I'll just go and put the kettle on.'

As she left the room she called back over her shoulder, 'Would you like a crumpet as well?'

'Yes please.'

Ten minutes later the pair of them were sitting sipping tea and nibbling crumpets that oozed with butter and homemade bramble jelly.

Tolstoy explained what he had been doing that afternoon. Elspeth listened intently and when he had finished she said, 'I think Hubert would have approved of your decisions over the club and ground. There is certainly a need for some new machinery and equipment. Hubert was feeling a bit guilty a couple of years ago, because he had meant to have a chat with Bert, but never got round to it. It certainly wasn't a matter of money, there was more than enough, but last winter, of course, he had the distraction of his diagnosis, so I doubt it would have crossed his mind. Anyway, in my opinion you've done really well, especially getting an offer of a discount from the locals. They have a fabulous reputation in the area, and they service the Manor's mowers and the chain saw, which Tommy the gardener organises for me. Anyway, it would seem that you have had a worthwhile day altogether.

'Now, what time have you ordered the taxi for?'

Tolstoy frowned, trying to remember. 'Um, seven. Then we drive round to Kate's to collect her.'

'Are you planning on having a shower beforehand?'

'Yes. Well as long as there's enough hot water.'

'Plenty.

'And what are you planning on wearing?'

'Well I'm not much of a tie person, so, open-necked shirt and my decent cords.'

'Good enough. But just to make sure I shall inspect you when you come downstairs, before you leave.' Tolstoy grinned at her. Elspeth was as good as her word when the spruced-up Tolstoy bounced down the main staircase an hour later, suited and booted, as it were. He ventured into the living room where Elspeth had been watching the television. She was absorbed in whatever the item was on the small screen and clearly had not heard Tolstoy come through the door. He cleared his throat politely and took a pace forward. Elspeth turned and, smiling, got to her feet. She had him blushing with her opening remark.

'Tolstoy, darling, you look delicious. Divine. Smart, but not too formal. Casual, yet not too relaxed. Now.' She approached him to inspect him more closely, then getting up on her toes and giving him the lightest of kisses on his right cheek, before brushing at the left shoulder of his jacket with the back of her right hand to get rid of a couple of hairs. 'A few words of advice, from a woman, me, which you can act on, or not, as you see fit. Remember to compliment her on how she looks within seconds of seeing her. Then, when you are chatting, let her do a lot of the talking and listen to what she says. Everything. And show an interest in it all. Ask her questions about her background – this is not just for you, but for me and the rest of the village gossips, since there is still much that we don't yet know about Kate. I want to know where she was brought up, what school she attended, and did she go to university? And if so, what did she read? In truth, these are all things that you need to know as well. Right, enough from me. I shall wait up for you, and please have a lovely evening.'

As he moved into the hall to collect his coat he heard the crunch of tyres on the gravel of the drive. The taxi had arrived, a couple of minutes early. Tolstoy was impressed. 'Taxi's here, Elspeth,' he called out. 'See you later.' With that he opened the door and stepped out into the chill evening, aware of butterflies in his stomach and his sweaty palms.

Unthinking he got into the front passenger seat of the taxi and gave Kate's address then settled back for the short drive to his date's cottage.

He practically leaped out of the car when it stopped at her gate and bustled up the path to her front door. There was an outside light under the roof of the minuscule porch, which made his search for a bell easier. He found no bell, so he lifted the old-fashioned knocker and let it drop heavily, making enough noise to rouse the whole village. Tolstoy had to wait for perhaps fifteen seconds, although, in his impatience to see Kate again, it seemed like an eternity to him before the door was opened. Kate stood there, backlit by the hall light and looking beautiful, he thought. 'Hi Tolstoy, I'll just get my coat,' and she turned and lifted a dark, woollen garment from behind the front door. Tolstoy remembered Elspeth's advice, and as they walked down the path together, he said, 'You look fantastic.'

She halted and turned to smile at him. 'Thank you, Tolstoy. You don't look too bad yourself.' He managed to reach ahead of her to flick up the gate latch and ushered her out to the waiting taxi. He opened the rear nearside passenger door for her, then closed it. He started to reach for the front door on the same side, when, in a moment of inspiration, he changed his mind and moved around the rear of the vehicle and got into the back seat on the other side. He felt rather pleased with himself at this manoeuvre, which found him sitting side by side with Kate.

'All set?' asked the taxi driver.

'Yes,' said Kate and Tolstoy in unison, and their first date had begun.

Elspeth was all agog when Tolstoy finally reappeared

shortly after eleven. He hung up his coat and went into the living room.

'So?' Elspeth raised an eyebrow. 'How did it go? No, wait. Tell me over a nightcap. What would you like? Wine? Whisky? Gin? A beer? Or even a cup of tea or a coffee?'

'I should like a glass of wine,' said Tolstoy. 'I think there's an unopened bottle in the fridge, isn't there?'

'That might now be an opened bottle, but there is certainly enough for a glass each,' said Elspeth, 'I opened it a little earlier.'

'OK, I'll be back in a mo,' said Tolstoy, heading for the kitchen.

On his return he poured out two generous glasses of white wine then settled on the sofa opposite Elspeth, who was in her favourite armchair.

It took some coaxing by Elspeth to find out how things had gone on the date, and when he was only halfway through his tale of the date they needed a refill, so Tolstoy headed down to the cellar for a couple more bottles.

The debriefing resumed. From what Elspeth could make out it had been an evening of ups and downs. Tolstoy explained that when they were shown to their table he somehow collided with the corner of a neighbouring table, hard enough to send a bottle of wine and one wine glass crashing to the floor, where wine was spilled amid shards of broken glass. Tolstoy naturally offered to pay for any cleaning, bought a replacement bottle for the couple, all the while apologising profusely. Kate was mute. Even frowning, he thought. Either embarrassed by him, or annoyed with him, he concluded. During the narration of this episode, Elspeth, for her part, had kept her face diplomatically expressionless, and made not a sound as he related the gory details of the start of his first date.

'Everything was eventually sorted out,' said Tolstoy, 'and we sat down opposite each other. But we hardly had any time to start chatting before the waiter came over with the menus and the wine list.' They studied the choices of food and drink, and having made their selections for each course, Tolstoy invited Kate to have a say in what wine they should drink, but she said that she was happy to drink whatever he ordered, informing him that she enjoyed both white and red, as well as rosé.

They placed their orders and Tolstoy apologised to Kate for the shambolic entrance, saying he was sure he had embarrassed and annoyed her.

'Oh Tolstoy, stop worrying about it,' she said. 'There's no point crying over spilt wine.' She paused and he suddenly grinned at her humour. 'To be honest I was just trying to keep a straight face. That's why I was frowning a little. And even you must admit it really was quite amusing. You had moved so carefully, and yet you still managed to catch that table.'

'The thing is,' said an embarrassed Tolstoy, 'I get these moments, when I seem to be so clumsy. I hadn't had an episode for a few months and I thought maybe I was over them, but this has just reminded me what an idiot I can make myself look.'

'You're not an idiot. Now put it to the back of your mind and let's enjoy the rest of the evening.'

Tolstoy assured Elspeth that he had followed her advice about listening to everything Kate said and asking her relevant questions. She had, for example, studied history of art at Leeds

University after attending a comprehensive school in the Midlands. Her father had died when she was at university, and her mother now lived in her native Scotland, in Fort William. She had one brother and one sister, both younger. She played the cello, or at least she used to. She enjoyed all music, but especially classical, and, unsurprisingly, loved art. She was a half-decent cook, and thought their meal that evening had been exemplary. 'And did she ask you about your background?'

'Yes,' replied Tolstoy. 'I gave her the short version. The long one is utterly boring.'

'Did you tell her you enjoyed music?'

'Yes, although a light sort of went out in her eyes when I mentioned jazz. But she did nod at me when I said I too like classical. I think though she prefers more modern classical. I told her Haydn was probably my all-time favourite composer and that I also liked music from the Baroque period. She didn't really react to that.'

'Were you still talking by the end of the meal?'

'Oh, yes. But just inconsequential things really. A bit of village chat. Thoughts on various locals. How well I've settled in here at the Manor. And, of course, the letter giving the Buttercup Field to the village. She said that when Wayne saw the documents he started nodding his head straightaway. She took that as a positive sign.'

'And when the taxi took you back to Kate's did you get out of the car and walk her to her front door?'

'Er... no. She had the door open far more quickly than I had anticipated. Said it had been a great evening and that she might see me in the pub tomorrow lunchtime. And thanks for taking her somewhere that produced such fabulous food. Then she shut the door and was gone.'

'Well, at least she was still talking to you at the end of the evening,' came Elspeth's response to counter Tolstoy's obvious disappointment. 'And it seems she wants to see you again, even if it is only at the old Snitcher's Head tomorrow. Perhaps, if you do bump into her in the pub, you could invite her around here for tea tomorrow afternoon. How does that sound?'

'That's not a bad idea. Maybe I will.'

Shortly after that he and Elspeth called it a day and headed off to bed, Tolstoy utterly drained by his busy day and his emotional evening. At least tomorrow, he thought, after switching off his bedside lamp, there was a chance of seeing Kate again.

ELEVEN

As things turned out, Tolstoy did not see Kate the following day. She made no appearance at the pub, much to his disappointment. He had even popped around to her cottage, but when he had knocked there was no one in to answer. The rest of the following week had him heading in multiple directions, not least because the driving school had mistakenly booked him in for a lesson every morning instead of arranging them for a fortnight hence. On the Monday he had been halfway through his boiled egg when the instructor knocked at the Manor door. So, having foregone the rest of his toasty soldiers, Tolstoy had sat behind the wheel of a car for the first time in his life. On hearing that he was such a neophyte, the instructor insisted that the first fifteen minutes or so be spent driving up and down the Manor driveway. Thankfully the car was an automatic. 'There is talk of a new model coming out that will have a self-drive mode,' the instructor announced to his pupil. 'Maybe I should wait until then,' said Tolstoy with a wry smile. Nevertheless, he gradually learned how to brake without sending his passenger flying into the windscreen. He also mastered throttle control, although at his first attempt he watched his foot on the throttle and forgot all about steering, until an alarmed cry from the instructor, followed by him stamping on the dual control brake, made Tolstoy look up. To his horror and embarrassment, had it not been for the instructor's quick thinking, Tolstoy realised the car would have slid into a shallow ditch that ran alongside the drive.

Despite the fact that it was not a public road, Tolstoy still had to deal with other vehicles. The first was Elspeth, returning from an early appointment with her hairdresser in Goudhurst. Tolstoy learned very quickly about getting into reverse, then swivelling to look over his left shoulder while still steering the car. 'Too many things to think about,' he thought to himself, as the car swerved this way and that along the drive until it reached the circular part where Elspeth could sweep around to her left and leave him a clear run up the drive again. He managed the manoeuvre a lot better a few minutes later, just after the instructor felt confident enough to entrust his vehicle and his life to his very inexperienced pupil. The car was just fifteen yards from the gateway when the postman's van swung in quite sharply. That required an emergency stop for Tolstoy, which he pulled off admirably, before demonstrating that his previous experience with Elspeth had taught him how to multi-task when reversing, although he still found the manoeuvre gave him a crick in the neck.

The rest of the lesson went far more smoothly, and the instructor recalculated how many lessons Tolstoy would require and concluded that he would be ready to sit his two-part driving test in the middle of January, provided he got in some extra practice between lessons. Elspeth later volunteered for this duty.

Thereafter it was a matter of squeezing in everything for the rest of the week. There was a fair amount of administrative and financial work to deal with, Tolstoy's income tax for starters, a review of what was being paid for heating oil, organising a surveyor to take a look at the cellarage, because Tolstoy felt it was damper than it should have been, the same expert to examine the roof, a job which Hubert had made sure was carried out every four or five years and Elspeth had told him it was now about time. There was also the painter and decorator to book, a chimney sweep, and around the grounds there was a definite need for some tree work. At some point Tolstoy wanted to firm up with Jack Bentley about permission to attend and, more importantly, to contribute to the plenary parish council meeting the following week. To that end he thought he might be advised to get in touch with Angela Smeaton; she would make a far more telling and convincing case when addressing the parish council than an amateur such as Tolstoy. So he then had to get contact details from the colonel for the two. He berated himself for failing to get the Stottenden Manor documents photocopied so that the colonel and Angela could have a chance to study them.

He was also still browsing equipment suppliers and sewage specialists on behalf of the cricket club. And he reminded himself to ask Bert for the name of a carpenter to build the sight screens and a professional to paint them. He was also trying to fit in the odd hour of extra driving with Elspeth, which meant he was taking her to the shops and back. All good experience, but time-consuming as well. By the end of the week he was feeling quite frazzled. At some point during the week he had had a brief phone call from Kate, firstly to apologise for not seeing him on the Sunday, the day after their first date, but she had had to visit a friend in London, who had a personal crisis, and two, that she was spending this weekend away at another friend's hen party, so Tolstoy's plans for Date Number Two went out of the window.

On the Friday evening he had a quick chat with Bert in the Snitcher's Head, and they agreed it would be a good idea for the two of them to pop down to the local agricultural engineers the following morning to start looking at mowers and rollers. Bert added that he had found a carpenter and a painter – both retired – who could help out for a very modest sum in each case, so that was the sight screens sorted.

They duly met up, with Bert driving on what was a very frosty Saturday morning, and there was good news at the engineers. Not only did they know of a privately owned Allen ride-on cylinder mower for sale, but it was in good condition, and although expensive, was not extortionately priced. The engineers said they would give it a thorough service, promising to repair where they could, otherwise they would replace, any parts that needed replacing. Finding a suitable roller was not quite so straightforward, but the engineers had some useful advice: contact councils and sports clubs to see if they had one they wanted to part with, or failing that, approach plant hire companies to see if they would be happy to sell on an older roller that was suitable for the cricket club's needs. All in all, Tolstoy felt rather pleased with the way things were developing, and on returning to the village, where Bert dropped him off at the pub, he treated himself to a quick and early pint of Fuggles. The only shadow to be cast on his day was in the form of Jack Bentley, at that moment the bar's solitary customer – other than the ever-present Old Ned, but that was a given as far as Tolstoy was concerned.

Nick Marten, the landlord, drew the pint. Tolstoy paid, then took a lengthy sip. Common courtesy demanded that he acknowledge the presence of one of his least favourite people, however. 'Morning, Jack.'

'Morning, Warren,' came the response.

'I was hoping to see you in here,' Tolstoy lied. 'When you present your find to the council members at next Thursday's meeting I wondered if I and a few other members of the Buttercup Field's action committee would be allowed to speak?'

'As long as it's not some sort of protest thing, with chanting when cabinet members are speaking. But what would you want to say, anyway?'

'Look at it as a courtesy. Since, as you rightly say, this discovery of the documents is almost certainly going to affect the village materially, then it would be only right and proper to give everyone, as well as the councillors, the opportunity to comment on the matter.'

'I suppose you have a point. OK, I'll make it clear at the start of the meeting that after the councillors have all had their say, that we will throw it open to the floor to give the villagers a chance to have their say, but they mustn't ramble on for too long.'

'Just make that clear to everyone when you lay down your ground rules,' said Tolstoy. 'Good, that's settled then. Cheers.' With that he drained his pint, dabbed his handkerchief over his upper lip to remove a moustache of froth that lingered there, then headed for the door. Having established the right to speak he needed to see the colonel and Angela. And fairly promptly. The previous evening the colonel had promised to do a ring around of the rest of the committee to apprise them of the discovery of the documents at Stottenden Manor and to ensure that as many as could turned up at the meeting in the village hall on Wednesday. And with luck, thought Tolstoy, the colonel had completed the task by now. It was quite a haul up the driveway to the colonel's impressive farmhouse. In fact, Tolstoy thought, farmhouse did not really cover it. It dwarfed Stottenden Manor, and he felt that stately home was nearer the mark. To his knowledge it had about a dozen bedrooms, endless reception rooms, a magnificent billiard room, imposing library, not to mention an enormous, and impressively well-stocked, wine cellar. And of course, there were outbuildings, a cottage or two and a couple of enormous barns as well as an unconverted oast-house. All in all, quite a property, more estate than farm.

Tolstoy was puffing a little by the time he arrived at the top of the drive, which at that point swept grandly around to the right to pass the front door and end in a generous parking area. In fact, the drive did not end there; there was a pair of wide farm gates which allowed the colonel access to the farmyard, which lay to the rear of the house, and, some four hundred yards distant, skirting the stunning formal gardens on which the colonel's wife lavished much love and attention.

Tolstoy climbed the five stone steps that were flanked by a stone balustrade, then approached the front door. Another outsized element, it had to be close on nine feet high. There was a rather modest bell-pull, on which Tolstoy tugged. He could hear nothing chiming, the door looked too thick to allow anything, let alone the sound of a doorbell, to pass through it, but about half a minute later it swung open and Miriam's smiling face appeared around it. 'Warren, what a lovely surprise. Do come in. Are you here to see Andrew?'

'Only for a couple of minutes. I'm sure he's rather busy.'

They moved across the generous hall, on one wall of which a large log fire blazed, and Miriam ushered Tolstoy into what she described as "the morning room", a beautifully-appointed, stunningly-proportioned room lined with bookshelves that were taller than Tolstoy. The shelves were lined with paperbacks, a couple of reference books and an impressive, if somewhat dated, collection of compact discs, things that had long since been rendered obsolete by technology.

'I'm afraid he's busy,' explained Miriam. 'Frightfully so. They had to cancel the shoot this morning after a really gory discovery. Harry Stoke got a call from Brian Marlow, our neighbour. He made a shocking discovery, that left even Harry looking a bit queasy.'

'What was it?'

'Well it sounds frightfully melodramatic, but Harry said that in this particular field, that runs alongside the public byway, were the heads and entrails of, I think he said, three of Brian's steers that were being readied for the Christmas market. Brian wondered if Harry or anyone who works on the shoot had heard or seen anything on the nightly patrols, and also if they had heard of any other farmer in this area having suffered the same thing. It is just perfectly frightful.'

'And *has* any other farmer suffered a similar crime?'

'We don't know, but Harry has promised to ask around, or "put out feelers", as he described it.'

'So these steers were slaughtered in the field, then? Is that what Harry thinks?'

'It seems to be the only logical explanation.'

'Well, it does sound awful. And poor Brian Marlow. No farmer can afford that kind of loss, I am sure, because I presume the steers would have been worth a fair amount to him, given the time of year.'

'Absolutely. It really is a horrid thing to have happened, and to such a nice man. So anyway, Andrew has been on the phone for the last hour or so, ringing around anyone and everyone who might have heard of a similar thing being carried out in another part of the county or the country. He says he thinks he saw a story in *The Times* or *The Telegraph* recently which reported a similar incident, but he can't remember where it happened, or when. Anyway, I'll just pop along to his study and let him know you're here.'

'Thanks, Miriam,' and Tolstoy began a tour of the bookshelves, intrigued to see what tickled the colonel's fancy on the reading front. To his surprise they were a mixed bag: lots of thrillers, but also books by food writers such as Elizabeth David, collections of recipes, some fairly old-looking volumes on what looked like fly fishing, as well as a number of larger format books on wine, champagne, claret, Burgundy and German wines being the dominant topics. But there were also a number of titles covering wines from Italy, Portugal, Australia, New Zealand, South Africa, North America and Canada. Tolstoy was impressed, and pulled out one on Bordeaux by Edmund Penning-Rowsell, a classic of its kind, and authoritative.

He began to read, and as ever, when he was reading, he was somehow able to shut out the world and become completely absorbed in the book, which was why he failed to hear the colonel entering the room.

'Ah, afternoon, Tolstoy.'

The reader looked up with a start. 'Andrew. Afternoon. Um,' he indicated the book on Bordeaux, 'I hope you don't mind me helping myself to a book. After what I inherited from Hubert I have become interested in wine, and I know next to nothing about claret, or any wine when it comes down to it.'

'You've no need to apologise. You're welcome to borrow it, although I would want it back. And when you've finished that one you can pick one on a different wine region, and gradually work your way through my modest collection. Now, I know you didn't come here to browse through my wine library, so what can I do for you?'

'I've just been having a chat with Jack Bentley and he has said that we'll be able to speak at the meeting. I didn't mention our set of documents, but I did say one or two of us might want to comment on Jack's announcement. I thought you ought to know, so that you can prepare yourself, and I'll now pop down to see Angela Smeaton so that she can also do some preparation. Obviously, there's not a lot we can do until we have the documents, but Kate has assured me that she should be getting them back either Tuesday or Wednesday. And I'll ring you the moment we have them.'

'Excellent news. Especially about being able to speak. Jack and the councillors will obviously be expecting to hear us objecting to their documents, when in fact we shall be producing the ones you found, plus certification of their authenticity.'

'Yes. But I don't think we are going to be the only ones speaking at the meeting. Bert Bryson gave me a heads-up in the pub, saying we should definitely be at the meeting, and he promised fireworks. I have no idea what's going on, but evidently something is going to happen. I hope it's not some sort of revelation about Jack's documents, which will be incontrovertible proof of his claims.'

'It all seems rather intriguing,' said the colonel. 'Now I'm afraid I have to go back to the phone. Miriam said she told you all about Brian's grisly discovery early this morning.'

'Yes. It sounds dreadful. It's not something I've ever heard or read about before.'

'I thought I'd give Brian a hand and offered to do some research to see if there have been similar incidents, and it turns out that this is not the first time this has happened. Apparently, there have been three other cases of on-the-spot slaughtering in the past fortnight. One was in East Sussex, the other two in Hampshire. In one of the Hampshire cases they killed six beasts. Oh and there was one incident that was reported a long time ago now, again in East Sussex, somewhere near Uckfield. I feel sorry for Brian. He works so hard. This must be quite a financial blow. So anyway, Tolstoy, I have to meet up with Brian shortly, but thanks for letting me know about speaking at the meeting, and if I don't see you before, then I shall see you there. It's a six-thirty start, I believe, in the village hall.'

By now they had moved into the hall and the colonel reached for the front door and hauled it open.

'Thanks, Andrew, and I shall take care of this,' Tolstoy indicated the book that he had tucked under his right arm. 'Thursday, if not before, bye.' And with that he set off down the drive and back to the road. The Smeatons lived in a detached Edwardian house along Back Lane, which ran behind the village shop and the pub. Tolstoy was feeling a trifle excited, and perhaps a little apprehensive. He was also anxious about the documents. He dearly wanted to have them in his possession now, not Tuesday or Wednesday. And he wanted them to be the real thing. What if they weren't? The real thing, that is. That was too awful to contemplate. He would feel humiliated. And he would have let down the whole village. He had felt a sense of responsibility from the moment he had moved into Stottenden Manor. It was almost proprietorial, not that he owned any part of the village beyond the Manor's grounds. Yet he had the cricket field, and that was a focal point for everyone. It held a place in their lives. And he desperately wanted the Buttercup Field issue to be resolved.

He walked up Back Lane then turned into the Smeatons' driveway. Not quite as grand as the colonel's, but there was still enough room for a modest sweep. He rang the bell and moments later Angela opened the door. 'Tolstoy!' she exclaimed. 'What a surprise! Come in.'

'I'd better not,' he replied. 'I'm running a little late and Elspeth is sorting out lunch for me. I just wanted to tell you that I met Jack Bentley a little earlier and he has said we can all speak at the meeting. I wanted to let you know so that you get a little preparation time.'

'Very good. Thank you, Tolstoy. Obviously, the sooner we have the documents back in our hands the better, though.'

'Yes, I do appreciate that. Kate reckoned Tuesday or Wednesday. I just hope it's the former. Right, I'm off. Oh, by the way, the meeting starts at six-thirty.'

'Thank you for letting me know. See you then.'

'Yes. Bye.'

As far as Tolstoy was concerned, the rest of the weekend just dragged by. With no Kate he couldn't even seek reassurance about the documents and their return. In the end, he immersed himself in the book on claret and let the weekend slide by at its own speed. He didn't even bother with a Sunday visit to the Snitcher's Head. He got his ration of exercise and fresh air by strolling around the cricket ground and the gardens of Stottenden Manor.

Monday found him edgy. Ever more apprehensive. The morning passed slowly. The afternoon, if anything, was even worse. That there was still no call from Kate left him worried. What if she and her forensic friend had miscalculated how long the process would take? He was tucking into crumpets and tea with Elspeth, late in the afternoon, when the phone rang. Elspeth stood and went over to the table where the phone lay. Tolstoy watched and waited, barely breathing, then he heard, 'Oh, hello Kate. How are you?' (a pause) 'Yes, he's here. Do you want to speak with him?' (another pause) 'Right, I'll hand you over. Tolstoy? It's Kate, for you.'

It was all he could do not to snatch the phone from Elspeth. But having managed to contain his impatience he greeted Kate. 'Hello. What news?'

'Wayne has completed the authentication of the documents and will be bringing them to Tunbridge Wells tomorrow. So I shall come to the Manor at about nine-thirty, if that's all right, and pick you up.'

'Yes. That's great. But what about the documents? Are they genuine?'

'Yes, they are. Isn't it wonderful?'

'Oh, that is the best news I've had in a long time. So we can now go to the council meeting on Thursday and end this whole sorry saga. What time is Wayne arriving tomorrow?'

'About eleven o'clock, or shortly after. We'll have time for some breakfast at a nice little place in the Pantiles, then it's a five-minute walk up to the station, where we'll be able to collect the documents from Wayne. Now, I'm sorry about this, but I have to go. I'm still at the shop and we have to close, then sort out the tills and everything. But I'll see you tomorrow morning, nine-thirty. Bye.'

'Bye, Kate, and thanks. See you in the morning.'

He hung up and placed the handset on the coffee table. 'That was Kate,' he said unnecessarily. 'We're meeting Wayne tomorrow in Tunbridge Wells, when we'll collect the documents. Kate's calling here to pick me up and we're going to have breakfast before meeting him at the station. But Kate says the documents are genuine. It's really great news. Now I can't wait for the council meeting.'

'Oh Tolstoy, that's wonderful,' said Elspeth, moving over to him and giving him a hug. 'It has made all those cobwebs and dust in the cellar well worth it. Are you going to ring Andrew to let him know?'

'Yes. And I'll also ring Angela Smeaton. She'll need to prepare her arguments. Oh, this is fantastic news!'

Tolstoy sat back, teacup in hand, somewhat dazed, but very happy, and he felt relief wash over him. Then excitement. He was thrilled. This should see off Jack Bentley and the council once and for all. And he and Kate were to have breakfast together tomorrow. And they would share the moment of collecting the documents. Double delight, he thought. Double delight.

When Kate called for him the following morning, Tolstoy was ready. He had to restrain himself from practically sprinting out of the Manor, forcing himself to turn around and check that he had closed the heavy oak front door, before walking briskly over to the car and letting himself in.

'Morning, Kate. Sleep well?'

'Morning, Tolstoy. Yes. You?'

'Like a hibernating bear. I now feel fully rested.'

'Weren't you a little excited about meeting Wayne today and picking up the documents?' Her tone was one of disappointment.

'Well, I knew the documents were genuine, because you told me on the phone yesterday evening. My only worry now is looking after them until the meeting, and beyond.'

They had left the Manor by then and were headed down the hill towards the main road. Kate glanced at him briefly, then back to the road ahead before saying, 'Yes. It's rather fun, isn't it? And I think you'll enjoy the breakfast, too. I often eat there first thing, sometimes even before I've opened the shop, although more usually once I have organised whoever is there to help me on that day.'

They had reached the junction and Tolstoy leaned back to give Kate a better view of the main road to the left, and decided not to say anything less it interfere with Kate's concentration. He had to admire the confident way she handled the car, and wondered if he would ever be as good. In fact, he wondered if he would even be able to pass his test.

'I think breakfast is my favourite meal of the day,' Tolstoy announced, once he felt it was safe enough, and that he wasn't going to distract Kate with his conversation. 'I do enjoy a cooked breakfast, although I make that a treat usually on a Sunday.'

'Do you go for a "full English", or do you just go with bacon and egg?'

'I suppose it's a sort of "full English", although I'm not too fond of black pudding, and I don't like tomatoes with eggs, I don't like what happens to the yolk. But I love bacon, good sausages, hash browns and mushrooms, and I prefer poached eggs to any other way of cooking them.'

'I'm rather conservative,' said Kate. 'I am quite happy with fried eggs, although I have a soft spot for scrambled eggs, as long as they are not boiled and turned into rubbery little balls. A friend's husband, who is a fantastic cook, adds a little grated parmesan to the mix and that adds a real "wow" to the eggs. I love bacon, but I'm not that crazy about sausages. Fried mushrooms are OK, though, and maybe the odd hash brown. What is the best breakfast you have ever eaten, or maybe I should ask, where was the best breakfast you have ever eaten?'

'That's easy. A place in Ireland, called Castlebar. I stumbled on a wonderful café early one morning and had the greatest bacon I've ever eaten anywhere. It was thick-cut, unsmoked, but the fat was crispy and the flavour was out of this world. On the menu of course it was called "The Full Irish", and it had everything, including black and white pudding. I ate the lot.'

'What were you doing in Ireland?'

'It was just after finishing at uni. A friend and I decided to walk from the east coast of Ireland over to the west coast.

We ended up in County Mayo, in Newport. Wonderful. Dramatic coastal scenery, there. Loads of little islands as well. We didn't stay anywhere near long enough.'

'I've never been to Ireland. I've often thought of going, but couldn't decide where. Dublin is an obvious place, but I like the countryside as well. I've toyed with the idea of taking the car from Donegal, right the way down the west coast and finishing up in Cork, or Waterford. But I'd have to have company. I'd be hopeless on my own in the car in a different country.'

'Maybe we should do that trip together,' Tolstoy blurted, instantly regretting opening his mouth. He gave her a sidelong glance to see if he had gone too far. But quite clearly he hadn't, because Kate's reaction, while unexpected, was a welcome one.

'That might be something to think about in the future. I think it's quite a good idea, but...' there just had to be a "but", thought Tolstoy, 'we'd have to wait until you've passed your test, because we'd have to share the driving.'

Tolstoy could not prevent a soppy grin from creasing his face. He failed to think of a single thing to say for a moment or two, therefore letting Kate continue, 'By the way, how are the lessons going?'

'Not bad. The first couple were a little hair-raising. I hadn't appreciated just how much is going on at the same time when you're driving. And I kept forgetting that I was in charge of it all, and allegedly had control, although that is a moot point based on those two lessons.'

Thereafter conversation skipped from one inconsequentiality to another until Kate found a parking place a short walk from the Pantiles. They were soon sitting at a table in a pleasant café in the historic quarter of Tunbridge Wells.

Breakfast was easy. 'Bacon, fried egg and toast for me,' said Kate, when a waitress arrived at their table, 'and a pot of tea.'

'The full Kentish for me, with a couple of rounds of toast, and coffee,' was Tolstoy's order.

'I think you'll like Wayne,' said Kate. 'He's a very down to earth sort of person, and very focused on his work. It wouldn't surprise me to learn that he has examined and tested the documents in his free time, to give himself something to do.' The tea and coffee arrived to provide a break in the conversation, Kate then picking up where she had left off. 'I used to feel sorry for his girlfriend, until he told me that she worked odd hours in a hospital path lab. They've been together for at least ten years that I know of, so they must be doing something right.'

'How old is he?'

'A tricky one. To look at he's late forties, maybe. Possibly early fifties. But to hear him talk, he can't be more than mid- to late thirties. He does have a gentle sense of humour, though. And he can laugh at himself, which I find an endearing trait in anyone.'

There was a pause as Kate took a sip of her tea. Tolstoy followed suit with his coffee, before throwing in a question that had clearly been bothering him.

'Have you any idea how much Wayne is going to charge?'

'No. Why? Are you worried about cost?'

'Oh, no, nothing like that. I only hope I have enough cash on me, that's all, otherwise I might have to slip up to a bank to use the cash machine.'

'I can probably lend you some money, from the shop's till, if you're desperate.'

'There's no need to do that. I'm OK for cash, it's just that I might need a bank. Is there one close by?'

'Not really. But let's cross that bridge when we come to it.'

The waitress then brought them their food, and for a short while the pair of them concentrated on eating. Kate then opened a new topic, speculating on how the council meeting would go.

Between forkfuls they imagined likely and unlikely scenarios, Tolstoy punctuating their chat with amusing comments about Jack Bentley, before they grew serious again.

'Supposing Jack really has a case,' mused Kate, 'how will we handle that?'

'I'm certain that Angela will cope brilliantly. She's a QC, after all. And from what I have gathered from Andrew and others in the village who know about these things, she is quite a renowned barrister.' He stopped suddenly, looking quizzical.

'Tolstoy, are you all right?' asked Kate, a thread of anxiety running through the six syllables.

'Well, I was just wondering, it's just me I'm afraid, I have odd thoughts from time to time, usually concerning words, and in this case I've just thought of something that has never occurred to me before.'

He paused long enough for Kate to ask, 'What have you just thought of?'

'Whether there is a female form of "barrister", just as you have an editor, and an editrix – the male and female forms, or a victor and a victrix.'

'So you are suggesting that it should be a "barristrix"? queried an incredulous Kate. 'You must be joking. Tell me you're joking, please. I've never heard anything so ridiculous.'

'Well,' said Tolstoy, 'it was just a thought, that's all. Just a harmless thought,' and he smiled at her.

They had finished eating and Tolstoy indicated he'd like the bill. He paid it, left a tip, helped Kate on with her coat and they headed off for the station. They had plenty of time, but it was a pleasant day and they felt no desire to hurry. Rather they opted for a gentle amble up the High Street.

Wayne's train did not keep them waiting too long. A chubby, greying man, with pale blue eyes and generous smile greeted Kate like the old friend she had clearly become. He shook hands with Tolstoy and handed over the documents to him.

'Yours, I believe. And very interesting too. You should have them preserved under glass cabinets for posterity, so that present and future generations can enjoy a serious piece of village history.'

Tolstoy was quite taken aback. 'What a good idea. Once this is all over I shall do just that. It will be something that the parish council might like to organise. Perhaps we could have an exhibition.'

'Or maybe they could be put somewhere prominent in the pavilion, since the Buttercup Field began its life as part of the cricket club,' Kate suggested.

'Another good suggestion,' said Tolstoy. He turned to Wayne. 'I'm sure you have no real interest in this discussion. What do I owe you for all this hard work?'

Wayne told him. A relieved Tolstoy was able to hand over the cash there and then, and while he did so Wayne explained, 'You have a certificate of authenticity, which my company is happy to issue. Should this go to court you'll find that the certificate will be accepted as a legal document. I would also be happy to appear as an "expert" witness. But I doubt it will come to that. I have included a full report on my findings and how I reached my various conclusions. I hope it does the trick for you.'

'I certainly hope so too, and thank you, Wayne, for all the trouble you've gone to, not just the work on the documents but coming down here each time to collect and deliver. I really appreciate it. You must come down with your wife, or partner, as my guest at the Manor. If you enjoy cricket, then we should make the date to coincide with a village home match. And then the four of us,' a sweeping arm brought Kate into the reckoning, 'could go out for a meal locally.'

'That sounds great,' said Wayne. 'I like cricket, and village cricket especially. I've even been known to wield a bat and sling a ball in my time.'

'Then perhaps we could squeeze you into the side,' said Tolstoy.

'No, I'd be happy just watching. Now look, I really have to go. More work waiting at the lab, and there's a London train leaving in ten minutes, so I'll head back, if that's OK. Look after those documents, won't you?'

Tolstoy assured him he would and they said their goodbyes.

'Right,' said Kate, 'time to get you back to Stottenden. Come on. We have a bit of a walk back to the car now. And I have to tell you, it's been an interesting, even a great, second date. Thank you for my breakfast, although I don't think I shall ever forget "barristrix"; it sounds more like a French cartoon character. Really! I must tell Angela.' And they headed off, Tolstoy holding the folder containing the documents firmly, but carefully, in one hand, petrified of dropping and damaging them. Kate meanwhile linked arms with his other one as they made their way back to the car.

TWELVE

The village hall was a hubbub of voices. Everyone talking at once, it seemed. Word had gone around Stottenden that something big was afoot on this foggy November evening. The Snitcher's Head had emptied at six-fifteen. The landlord, Nick Marten, ever a practical man, had shut up shop temporarily and had joined the throng as it made its way to the parish council meeting. The whole complement of the action committee was there; the Reverend Davis with his wife Suzanne, Jo, Harry, all the local farm workers. *In fact*, thought Tolstoy, looking around at the packed hall, *I doubt if there is anyone left at home this evening*. There was a real tingle to the atmosphere. Kate, standing, pressed against Tolstoy, felt it and glanced up at his flushed face. She smiled.

It really was a bit cramped. He spotted Bert, together with Old Ned, standing close to the "top" table, which in fact was three trestle tables arranged to accommodate the councillors on the small stage at one end of the hall. Actually, to call it a stage was to exaggerate. It was no higher than nine inches, running the width of the hall and perhaps occupying a total of ten feet. It scarcely elevated the councillors above the plebiscite. Jack Bentley was at the head of the table, with councillors ranged down the two long sides, three on one side, two on the other, with the final place being at the opposite end to the chairman. There was also a well-dressed man, in suit and collar and tie, sitting alongside, but slightly behind, Bentley. He was clutching a briefcase and managed to look self-important. *Must be the solicitor*, thought Tolstoy. And at the back of the raised area Tolstoy spotted the two farmhands who worked for Bentley.

At that moment Bentley called the meeting to order. He glanced at the agenda and they were off. The minutes of the previous meeting were approved without demur. No matters arising from said minutes, they moved to item one, and, as it turned out, the only item on the agenda. 'I should perhaps, at this point, declare an interest,' Bentley addressed the floor. 'However, since everyone here also has an interest in item one, the discovery of historic documents concerning the Buttercup Field and the holder of title to the plot, if it is all the same to everyone, I shall remain in the chair and introduce the matter. There will be an opportunity for questions and comments later, these to put through me. Thank you.'

He cleared his throat, took a sip of water from a plastic bottle that had been placed on the table in front of him, looked down at a sheaf of papers in his hands, then began.

'Approximately two weeks ago my attention was drawn by two of my farm labourers, that one of the gateposts of the roadside entrance to the Buttercup Field had developed a wobble. Not wanting anything untoward to happen to anyone using the gate to access the Buttercup Field,' he paused, and it quickly became evident that he had done so in order to emphasise the next statement, 'I instructed my men to repair the gate. I decided not to refer this job to the council, but rather I made the decision to pay for the costs of the job out of my own pocket.' Another pause, greeted with dead silence in the hall.

Bentley grunted, then continued, 'I now call Clem Pewsey, one of my most senior labourers, to step forward and relate to this meeting what happened when he and his colleague, Scott Ritching, began digging. Clem!' he called and the elder of the two men shuffled self-consciously to the table.

'OK, Clem, take your time, and tell this meeting what happened.'

There was a great deal of throat-clearing by Bentley's employee, who was wheezing terribly, but eventually, after a couple of false starts, and a table of "ums and ers" he finally managed to get out the details. 'We'd taken the gate off its 'inges, and we was digging around the base of the 'inge post when the spade 'it summat. We couldn't budge it with the spade, so thinking 'twere a rock or a large stone at least, we decided to use the crowbar. 'Twas Scott who drove the bar straight down. That's when we realised 'tweren't no stone, cos we 'eard the sound of wood splintering.' There was a chuckle from Scott backstage, as it were, and an accompanying couple of sniggers from the floor. Clem waited a few seconds then carried on with his report. 'Once we cleared the dirt away we found we was looking at an old box.'

At this point Bentley just could not contain himself. 'And what was in the box?'

'Well, sir, earth, you know, dirt from where the spade 'ad made a 'ole in the lid, like.' There were louder, more widespread chuckles throughout the hall.

'Yes, yes, all right,' snapped Bentley, irritated to have been made to look a little foolish, 'but what else was in the box?'

'Well, sir, papers. Old papers, with writing on them.'

'And what did you do when you found these papers?'

'Well, sir, we brought them to you.'

'Thank you, Clem. That's all we need from you.' He turned portentously to the villagers, paused melodramatically, then said in as solemn a voice as he could manage, 'These papers, which I have here, in front of me, are proof that the Buttercup Field was given to my grandfather Edwin Bentley by Hubert de Groot's grandfather, Cornelis, in 1895. And here is the proof.'

Triumphantly Bentley selected some sheets of paper, then waved them above his head. This prompted mutterings, that became louder when Bentley continued, 'This is proof that the land belonged to my family. I am therefore legally empowered,' he turned to the smartly-dressed man sitting alongside him, as if for confirmation, 'to donate the land to the council, which can now go ahead and develop the Buttercup Field.'

At this, the mutterings became an angry growl. Fists were being shaken in the direction of the stage. And words such as crook, cheat, and land-grabber were directed in Bentley's direction.

It was a question, shouted from the front of the simmering throng, and shouted forcibly, before being repeated a number of times, which gradually caught the attention of everyone in the hall.

It was Old Ned, speaking more loudly than anyone could remember. 'Clem? Can you tell me what you was doing back in Feb'ry, when I 'eard you wheezing away, while you was digging at that very gate where you "discovered" this box of documents? It was just after midnight. I was 'avin' my usual sit-down under that old oak tree in the Buttercup Field an' I 'eard you and another person, who I reckon 'ad to be young Scott there, whispering to each other, then the sound of digging. And I 'ave to say Clem, there is no chance it was anyone else, because not even my old car wheezes as loud as you do.' That got a laugh from the audience, who had been hanging on to Ned's every word.

''Tweren't I,' spluttered Clem. 'Last February? I can't remember what I was doing last week or last night. But I do know I weren't digging.'

'Oh yes you was,' Ned countered. 'I went back the following morning and blow me down if the 'inge post didn't 'ave fresh dirt packed around it. And another thing, I was leaning on that very gate on the morning you say you found it wobbling, and it was solid as the day it was sunk into the soil by my old dad. Wobble, my arse. The only thing wobbling was you, after too much beer. I never 'eard such nonsense. You put that box in the dirt back in Feb'ry, no doubt under instruction from Mr Jack Bentley, and it was then left until the time seemed right to produce it like a rabbit out of a 'at.'

Old Ned paused dramatically, and for a few seconds his last words seemed to hang over everyone.

Pandemonium followed. There was uproar in the hall. Clem was applying his inhaler, while a very red-faced Jack

Bentley was trying to regain control of events. Eventually Angela Smeaton, who had been standing alongside Old Ned, stepped up onto the stage. All it took from her was a raised hand and within seconds silence returned.

'Jack,' she began in a voice of reason, 'I'm sure there is an explanation for all of this, because these are serious allegations. May we see these documents?'

'Yes, of course, but handle them carefully.'

'Oh I most certainly will.' With that she pulled on cotton gloves.

'Why are you putting on gloves? Afraid of getting your hands dirty?'

'No, Jack, not at all. I just don't want to add my fingerprints to those that are already on these documents, which will include yours, of course, your solicitor's, Clem's, not to mention those of Cornelis and your grandfather. I am sure you understand that the action committee cannot just accept these documents at face value. We must have them checked forensically, and have them authenticated.'

'What? What? Don't be ridiculous! There's no need for all that fuss. One glance at them tells you they are genuine.'

'I'm afraid I have to tell you that I am no expert, but nor was I born yesterday. I must insist that these documents be analysed and assessed and authenticated before they can be accepted as genuine. Fingerprinting, dating of the ink, dating of the paper, comparison of the English used with similar documents from the same period, all of that can, and will, have to be carried out if you want this village to accept them as the real thing and thus allow you and the council to build anything on the Buttercup Field.'

She paused. No one said a thing. Jack Bentley had gone pale. His mouth had twisted into a grimace, but there was something akin to fear in his eyes.

Angela swished aside an imaginary robe, before continuing, 'If you need to use a forensic laboratory I am sure Warren Pearce here,' she paused to indicate Tolstoy, 'could recommend one. The forensic laboratory which Warren approached has just done a wonderful job for him, verifying and authenticating documents he has uncovered in the cellar of Stottenden Manor. Their fees were very reasonable, weren't they Tolstoy?'

She had turned again to single him out, waited for him to nod, then, smiling, she turned her steely gaze back on Jack Bentley. 'Are you interested in hearing about the documents that Tolstoy discovered, Jack?'

Jack Bentley's face now wore a puzzled look, one also evident on many faces among the audience, including those of the councillors.

'I shall take your silence as an affirmative response to my question. The documents that Tolstoy unearthed date from 1839,' she looked up sharply at a now rapidly deflating parish council chairman. Angela then rummaged through her briefcase and brought out the file folder containing the ancient legal envelope, then carefully she manipulated its contents, eased them out and, stepping forward, placed them on the table.

'Now where is the bit I want?' She pretended to riffle through the documents, before extracting two and exclaiming, 'Ah yes! Here we are. This is from the de Groot family's firm of solicitors in Tonbridge, still in practice now too, I believe. It is dated November 14th, 1911.' And dramatically she began to read. '*Dear Cornelis, Please find enclosed the documents you requested. You may keep them, unless you would prefer to return them to our sturdy office safe. The two relevant plans you felt sure were included among the deeds to Stottenden Manor were indeed there and they are self-explanatory. One is dated before, the other after, the changes were made. Your grandfather, Willem, clearly created a smaller field as some sort of shield from the road, to help enclose the cricket ground.*' Angela paused and looked up at Bentley, who by now had slumped in his seat. 'There is actually a fair bit of correspondence between the solicitor and Cornelis de Groot, and that could prove useful right now, this evening, because we could do a quick comparison of the handwriting, to verify that Cornelis really did hand over the title of the Buttercup Field to your grandfather. If the handwriting in these documents,' she indicated the Manor's paperwork, 'matches that which is in yours, then perhaps you will have a case. However, I would caution against fighting it, even if there is a match, because there is enough written evidence here to say that in fact Cornelis was in no legal position to have handed over the land to your family, since it had already been handed over to the church, here in Stottenden, more than half a century earlier, in 1839 to be precise.'

Bentley looked stunned.

'So, Jack, could you please let me have a copy of the letter you claim is from Cornelis to your grandfather so that I, and others, including of course, yourself, may make the comparison of the handwriting?'

There was a breathless hush in the hall. For those in the know, Bentley was going to lose a great deal, because there was little chance he could have imitated the handwriting of

Cornelis de Groot, so his choice, was, as the popular press would have it, stark. Hand it over and be found out, or refuse to allow the comparison and concede that the Buttercup Field did belong to the church, and by extension, the village.

All eyes were on Jack Bentley. He ran an anguished hand through his slicked-back hair and looked around wildly. He saw nothing. No allies. No sympathy. There was curiosity, that was just about the only thing visible on the faces of everyone. Curiosity as to what would happen now.

Finally, after what had seemed like hours but in reality was a bare half-minute, Bentley got to his feet, pulled his documents to him, gathered them up and folded them, before slipping them into his inside jacket pocket. Then, in a voice that suddenly sounded like that of a very old man, he said, quaveringly, and for many, unconvincingly, 'Quite obviously in the light of these revelations about an earlier agreement involving the Buttercup Field, the papers that I hold in my hand, while being genuine, have no legal standing. They have been pre-dated by very many years. The gift had already been made. Since my family has done without the Buttercup Field for all this time anyway, there is nothing lost to us. I therefore withdraw the planning application. The Buttercup Field belongs to the church, and as Angela said, by extension to the village. Thank you.'

He started to move away from the table as loud cheers hailed the announcement, but Angela stopped him in his tracks. 'Jack,' it came out quite sharply, 'there is more to come and you have not formally closed the council meeting.' She turned to the main hall and appealed for quiet. 'Please, everyone, just a few more minutes of your time, then the celebrations can begin.' Silence fell. Bentley moved back to his chair, nodded at his fellow councillors, then invited Angela to continue.

She addressed her remarks to the councillors. 'I have here two original plans of the cricket field before and after the gift was made to the church, with the statement on one from Hubert de Groot's great-great-grandfather, Willem, that he had made the new field over to the church of St Martin for use by the village and villagers in perpetuity. All these documents are accompanied by a certificate of authenticity from a respectable forensic laboratory in North London. I would formally request the parish council, and its leader, Jack Bentley, to acknowledge acceptance of these documents and their authenticity, and to declare that the proposals to build on the Buttercup Field will now be shelved for good.' More cheers broke out, but again, an elegant wave of a hand by Angela hushed the hall.

Jack Bentley stood up and, with a degree more formality than might have been expected, said, 'Stottenden parish council hereby accepts the authenticity of the documents which will prevent any building or development work to be carried out on the piece of land known as the Buttercup Field in perpetuity. The planning application for residential development is hereby withdrawn.' He then turned to the clerk of the council and asked for that statement to be minuted as well.

Cheering once more broke out, but this time the cheers were more for Angela Smeaton and her brisk demolition of Bentley's case. During a brief break in the celebrations Bentley formally asked if there was any other business. On discovering there was none he formally closed the meeting, then, for the second time that evening, pushed back his chair, got to his feet and gathered up his papers. This time he was allowed through, the crowd parting to create a passage for him. Once he was clear of the crowd and heading towards the front door of the hall everyone closed ranks again and rushed towards the stage, where Angela was being alternately hugged and patted on the back for her handling of the case.

Tolstoy and Kate had managed a hug and a peck on each other's cheeks. Elspeth wiped a tear from her eye, grateful that her husband's legacy would live on. Grateful, too, that Tolstoy had been the one to discover the documents. Bert was seen to slap Old Ned on the back and then guide him to the hall door, whence they would make their way to the Snitcher's Head. Nick Marten had already left, together with Jo, to prepare for what promised to be quite a busy night. For a couple of minutes everyone else just milled around, smiling, laughing, punching the air, before someone realised that the pub would now be open, and the crowd as one, surged towards the exit, their minds focused on a celebratory drink.

When the bulk of the villagers had gone, leaving only Angela, her husband Bertie, the colonel, his wife Miriam, Elspeth, Kate and Tolstoy, the seven of them heaved a collective sigh of relief.

'Angela, thank you,' said the colonel. 'First-rate job. Best bit of advocacy I've ever witnessed. In boxing terms, you had him on the ropes and then on the canvas. He never stood a chance. The pity of it is that we didn't get to see his "evidence", although that was an inspired tactic to say we could do a direct comparison of handwriting right then and there. That surely would have shown him up for what he is, a shyster and a fraud. That was a truly magnificent job. Again, thank you.'

'Thank you for your kind words, but I think Tolstoy here also deserves our gratitude. After all, if he hadn't braved the dust of a couple of centuries and then patiently waded through what I gather were reams of old papers, then none of this could have taken place, and we would be in the Snitcher's Head right now, but drowning our sorrows, rather than celebrating a victory. And worse, the council and Mr Jack Bentley would even now be driving the diggers and dumper trucks onto the Buttercup Field. Andrew, your role in this has been no less important. You brought everyone in the village – apart from Bentley and his henchmen – together. It meant the villagers were able to put up a united front, and as we have seen this evening, they are overjoyed at the outcome. Now I suggest we all join them and have a drink or two to celebrate a famous victory. Shall we go?' And taking her husband's arm Angela swept towards the door with the others bringing up the rear.

Loud cheers greeted the seven as they made their way to the bar. Nick Marten had declared that the first three rounds were on the house, and Old Ned had already drained his first glass and was eyeing up his second pint of cider. Bert was standing by him, sipping a little more judiciously at his pint of Fuggles.

Tolstoy squeezed through happy bodies, heading over to the corner where Old Ned held sway. On arriving there he tapped Ned on the shoulder and said, 'That was magnificent, Ned, thank you. Even before Angela hit him with all our documents you had knocked the stuffing out of Jack. It was so unexpected, and frankly it won the day for us.'

'I agree, wholeheartedly,' came a voice over Tolstoy's shoulder. It was Andrew. 'That was something that came out of left field. You really shook old Clem, and it was patently obvious thereafter that he and Scott had planted that box by the gatepost on instructions from Jack Bentley.'

Old Ned was flushed with pride at the comments from the two of them. He smiled, a little lost for words, then picked up his glass and raised it to them. They all took a sip from their own.

Then Tolstoy asked Ned, 'Why is it called the Buttercup Field? Was it once carpeted with buttercups, until disease or whatever wiped them all out?'

A wicked smile crept across Old Ned's face. He slowly shook his head. 'No,' he said, 'the Buttercup Field weren't named after they bloody weeds. No buttercup has ever grown there. Remember, 'twas part of a larger field that were mown and tended right well, even back in them days. No, 'twas named the Buttercup Field by my great-uncle Ted and 'is mates when they was teenagers. 'Im and 'is mates called it the Buttercup Field like a sort of disguised name for the place. A code, if you like. Because, you see,' he lowered his voice and leaned towards Tolstoy and the colonel, 'come the longer evenings of spring and summer, after a hard day's labouring in the fields, the young 'uns 'ould make their way to the Buttercup Field, which was, by then, screened from prying eyes in the pub and the big house by the 'edges and trees wot 'ad grown up there. The grass were deliberately left long in the field. And the young lads and their girls 'ould get down and do what Mother Nature intended. Now when that were all goin' on, if you were to look across the field with up to half a dozen couples doin' it, all you could see

198

were the backsides risin' and fallin'. An' that's when Uncle Ted and 'is mates decided they'd give the field a name, but not the Bums Up Field, that 'ould be too obvious, an' a mite rude. No, they thought they could make it sound innocent. So, what everyone 'eard was the youngsters calling it "the Buttercup Field", but in reality they was callin' it "the Buttock Up Field".'

ACKNOWLEDGEMENTS

Had it not been for the rain at Taunton during a Somerset match in 1990 this story would never have been started, let alone completed – albeit 29 years later. My first thank-you, therefore, must go to the late Eric Hill, who came up with the idea of someone inheriting a cricket ground, while rain trickled down the windows of the old press box.

Mention also has to be made of the people, friends and family, who bravely read through the raw manuscript making corrections, suggestions and never once complaining. So thank you Audrey King, Colin Bateman, my sister Sarah Gillett and my brother Glyn Llewellyn.

The cover is the work of Dr Linda King, another long-standing friend, who allowed herself to be persuaded to put paintbrush to paper and capture the rural idyll that I have tried to depict in this book. She succeeded, and the book is all the better for it.

The team at Matador, most notably Fern Bushnell, the company's Production Controller, Alexa Davies, Lauren Bailey, Hannah Dakin, Hayley Russell and Andrea Johnson, has been exemplary. Everyone of them has bent over backwards to help me, often going beyond the bounds of duty. Their patience and professionalism cannot be faulted.

Finally, my deepest gratitude goes to my long-suffering wife Hilary, who has had to read and re-read every attempt to start this work, and those attempts are many, then finally reading and making positive criticism of the completed novel over the last 29 years.